Praise for Jessica James' Books

"Very engaging. Hard to put down."
— BILLY ALLMON, U.S. Navy SEAL (Retired)

"Sweetly sentimental and moving... An endearing page-turner."
— PUBLISHERS WEEKLY

"A tapestry of emotion deeply set inside the bravest of Americans: the soldier."
— MILITARY WRITERS SOCIETY of AMERICA

"Reminds me of *American Sniper* and *Lone Survivor*, but accompanied with a beautiful and epic romance that is completely unforgettable."
— LAUREN HOFF, United States Air Force

"Spot on with characters and descriptions. Strong women. Larger than life men. Well done."
— LYNNETTE BUKOWSKI, Founder/CEO of LZ-Grace Warriors Retreat Foundation and Ombudsman to Special Operation NSW Commands

"A heart-rending, white-knuckle journey into the courageous lives of our nation's heroes. Shows us the meaning of commitment—to country, and to love."
— JOCELYN GREEN, Award-winning author

Other Books by Jessica James

Romantic Suspense
DEAD LINE (Book 1 Phantom Force Tactical - The Prequel)
FINE LINE (Book 2 Phantom Force Tactical)
FRONT LINE (Book 3 Phantom Force Tactical)

Meant To Be: A Novel of Honor and Duty

Historical Fiction
Noble Cause (Book 1 Heroes Through History)
(An alternative ending to Shades of Gray)

Above and Beyond (Book 2 Heroes Through History)
Liberty and Destiny (Book 3 Heroes Through History)
Shades of Gray: A Novel of the Civil War in Virginia

Non-Fiction
The Gray Ghost of Civil War Virginia: John Singleton Mosby
From the Heart: Love Stories and Letters from the Civil War

www.jessicajamesbooks.com

Book 2
Phantom Force Tactical

FINE LINE

#DASH: Dare All For Sacred Honor

Jessica James

ISBN 978-1-941020-11-1
Library of Congress Control Number: 2016912592

Edited by Literally Addicted to Detail Services
Cover Design: Redbird Designs
Interior Design: Patriot Press

September 2016

Proudly Printed in the United States of America

Vincent amor patriae

"The love of country conquers."
— Virgil

Prologue

Blake Madison reached for the alarm at the first ding so it wouldn't wake his wife.

"It's Saturday," Cait said sleepily, reaching for his arm. "Sleep in."

"I'm going for a quick run." He crawled out from under the covers, carefully moving their ninety-five-pound German shepherd, Max, off his legs. "It's a lot of pressure having a young trophy wife. I have to stay in shape."

She threw a pillow at him, but then reached over and ran her hand over his abs. "You're doing a pretty good job. Feels like the body of a young Navy SEAL."

He laughed. "Young? No. SEAL? Not anymore." Then he leaned in close. "How do you know what the body of a young Navy SEAL feels like anyway?"

Her lips broke into a smile even though her eyes were closed. "Just guessing. Don't worry, I prefer the old, retired model."

"Good answer. I *think*." Blake got up and fumbled around in the dim light to find a pair of sweatpants and a tee shirt. After getting dressed, he had almost reached the door when he heard a voice from beneath the covers.

"You forgot something."

He came back and bent over Cait. "I know. But I was

afraid I'd be tempted to crawl back into bed."

"Good answer. I'm *sure*." She reached up, grabbed a handful of his shirt, and pulled him down for a kiss, causing him to linger.

With his hands propped on each side of her pillow, he stared into her eyes. "Do you know how much I love you, Mrs. Madison?"

She grinned sleepily and pulled him close again. "Show me."

He sighed. "I just did that a few hours ago. Remember?"

"Umm hmm." She drew the words out with her eyes still closed and a contented smile on her face. "But that was last night."

He glanced at the door, then back at the bed.

She must have sensed his hesitation. "I'm just kidding. We have all day. Go for your run."

Blake lifted her hand off the covers and kissed it. "We've been married almost a year. We need to start acting like an old married couple, not newlyweds."

Caitlin opened one eye momentarily. "Are you saying you want me to become a nag?"

"Only if you nag me about getting back into bed with you."

He gave her another long kiss and then stood and stared down at her in the dim light. She was wearing his NAVY tee shirt—or as she called it, her favorite negligée—with the pearl necklace he'd given her the night before contrasting brightly against the dark blue. His gaze shifted to the wedding band on her hand and then drifted to her tousled hair spread out on the pillow, and her long lashes resting on her cheeks. He reconsidered his need for outdoor exercise.

"Bring me a cup of coffee when you get back," she murmured, pulling the covers up and rolling over.

"I won't be long, baby." He headed toward the door and patted his leg for the dog to follow. "I'll take Max so you don't have to get up and let him out."

"Love you."

His heart flipped. "Love you more."

Just as he started to close the door, she spoke again. "Don't miss me too much."

He grinned as the door clicked shut. She always said that when he left, even if they were only going to be separated for a few minutes. It had become a routine. Even the kids said it now when they left for school or went to visit a friend. *Don't miss me too much, Daddy.*

Heading down the stairs, he turned off the security alarm and went out onto the porch, taking a deep breath of the cool morning air. After doing a few stretches, he sprinted down the gravel lane, his heart bursting with happiness and contentment. Until recently, Blake had been blind to the beauty of the scenes that surrounded him; now, he felt as if he were seeing the world through fresh eyes that noticed the gifts that had always been right in front of him.

He knew there was only one reason for that—and that reason was lying in the bed upstairs, waiting for him.

As he listened to the cadence of his feet hitting the dirt road and the sound of his steady breathing, his mind drifted to his upcoming wedding anniversary. He wanted to come up with something really special to celebrate—something that would show Cait how much she meant to him and the kids. It had been on his mind for weeks, but now the milestone moment loomed just days away, and he still didn't know what that *something* was.

It had to be a gift that was special and personal, one unique enough to make Cait understand the depths of his affection. The pearl necklace he'd given her the night before as an "early present" had made her squeal with surprise and delight, but that was the kind of thing every husband got his wife.

Cait was different. Their circumstances were different. Although their marriage was a happy one, the months that had passed since they'd said their vows had not all been easy ones. Lots of changes had come about—some had tested their relationship, others had strengthened it. The fact that Cait had given up a successful journalism career to concentrate on becoming a wife to him and a mother to his children was a testament to her commitment. She had poured her heart and soul into making his life perfect. But he knew that choice had been a tougher adjustment than she let on.

Blake had made significant changes too, quitting his job as a homicide detective to fulfill a dream of starting his own company with his best friend Nicholas Colton, a former SEAL teammate. Called Phantom Force Tactical, the firm provided high-threat protective detail to government and civilian VIPs, and could deliver counterterrorism and assault capabilities both overseas and in the United States. Although relatively new, Phantom Force had already inked contracts with a handful of Fortune 500 companies to provide bodyguards, weapons training, and security consultations all over the world. Just yesterday he'd gone to DC to submit paperwork for a contract to provide protection for U.S. Embassies and Consulates abroad. If they got the deal, Phantom Force would have the footing to compete with just about any defense agency in the world.

Bypassing the security gate for vehicles he'd installed, Blake turned left at the end of their long driveway and continued on the dirt road toward the main thoroughfare. The gate seemed out of place in this peaceful country setting, but had become necessary after he and Cait had exposed a scandal at the U.S. State Department. They'd tried to keep a low profile and return to their private lives, but the press reports and social media campaigns from political fanatics made that impossible.

After receiving some intimidating communications and a few death threats immediately following the hearings, Blake had taken the extra steps of installing the electronic gate to stop vehicles, and upgraded the security system in the house. It was fairly low-level—just alarms on the doors and windows if anyone tried to break in, and a few security cameras. Cait had insisted on keeping it simple. She didn't want to allow fear or intimidation to control their lives.

Blake glanced down at Max, who trotted contentedly beside him. The dog had been one security measure Cait had not argued about. In fact, it hadn't taken Max long to move from protector to pet—Cait's pet. Max followed her everywhere, including their bedroom. The longstanding house rule that dogs didn't sleep on beds had been reluctantly withdrawn by the second week. Blake consoled himself with the knowledge that the connection between Cait and Max meant no one was going to get out of their house alive if the dog thought her life was in danger.

Not that Blake worried about Cait's security very much. She was a strong, independent woman, who had gone head-to-head with some of the most dangerous and powerful figures in the country. She knew how to protect herself, and took great pride in being able to compete with him and his men on the firing range.

The large parcel of property they lived on had the added security measure of being a hangout for his former Navy SEAL buddies and other special operators. Some would stop by for an hour to drink a beer; others would stay a few days to unwind. Plans were in the works to build some small cabins to house the men in between deployments, but a firing range and storage building for vehicles and weapons had taken precedence over that. The twenty-five-yard pistol range and one hundred-yard machine gun range were now in full operation, so they could begin to concentrate on the next phase.

With his breath coming faster now, Blake slowed his pace slightly. He inhaled the musty smell of dying leaves and contemplated the gold and red colors splashed like a painter's canvas all around him. It was his favorite time of year. Warm days. Cool nights. Cloudless blue skies and star-filled heavens. He'd worked hard to hold on to this family home so his children could grow up in this small slice of paradise. Although the hustle and bustle of DC was less than an hour away, this world consisted of dirt roads and hundreds of acres of fields and woods.

And it was profuse with history. His great-grandmother, Alexandria Hunter, had inherited the huge estate from her grandmother, Andrea Hunter, wife of the notorious Confederate cavalry officer Colonel Alexander Hunter. During and immediately following the Civil War, Hawthorne, as it was known, had been an active horse breeding farm. Over the years, parcels had been sold off, but the estate still consisted of two hundred and fifty acres of rolling hills and pastureland.

Passing the three-mile mark he knew by heart, Blake picked up his pace again. But just a few strides later, the image of Cait lying in bed pulled at him like a magnet, causing him to turn around before he'd made it to the main road. If the kids were still asleep, maybe he'd take a quick shower and rejoin her.

Sprinting the last hundred yards, Blake was surprised when Max didn't follow him up the porch but continued around the side of the house with his nose to the ground. The dog usually had a hearty appetite after a run and wanted to be fed immediately.

"Where you going, boy? Smell a raccoon or something?"

Blake let him go and entered the house to find his daughter, Whitney, walking slowly down the stairs, looking disheveled but wide awake.

So much for going back to bed.

"What are you doing up so early, young lady?"

He didn't hear her answer as he continued into the kitchen, humming *Oh What a Beautiful Morning* from the show *Oklahoma.* He shook his head to rid it of the song.

Geez. If Colt heard me humming that, I'd never hear the end of it.
He couldn't help it. The sound of Broadway show soundtracks blaring from the house was a common occurrence since Cait had moved in. Blake wouldn't admit it to anyone, but he probably knew every word to *Camelot* and *Phantom of the Opera*, two of her favorites.

After turning on the coffee pot, he stood in the glow of the open refrigerator door, trying to figure out what he could scrounge up. Maybe he'd surprise Cait with breakfast in bed as another early anniversary gift.

Whitney shuffled into the room behind him in her big pink slippers and noisily pulled out a chair at the small kitchen table. "When is Cait coming back, Daddy?"

"What, honey?" Blake continued staring into the fridge. Having just turned four, Whitney talked a lot, but didn't always make sense.

"When are those men bringing her back?"

Even before Blake could resolve in his mind what she'd said, his body responded as if he'd just heard the click of a trigger shattering the stillness of a dark night—and within the span of a heartbeat, the small twinge of alarm ignited into an urgent need to react. He closed the refrigerator door slowly, reminding himself to appear calm, even though the high-octane dose of adrenaline pulsing through his veins was making it difficult to breathe, let alone think. He turned to Whitney and knelt down beside her. "What men, honey? What are you talking about?"

"The mean ones." Her eyes brimmed with tears.

Blake didn't ask any more questions. He stood and turned

in one movement.

Racing to the stairs, he took them two at a time and headed at a full sprint down the hallway to the master bedroom.
He tried to enter the room quietly, but almost tore the door
off its hinges in his urgency.

The bed was empty.

Chapter 1

Nicholas "Colt" Colton sat straight up from a deep sleep and reached groggily for his phone. After squinting at the name on the screen and then the time of day, he answered.

"This better be good, bro."

"Cait's gone."

"Don't worry, she loves you. She'll come back. They always do." He squinted again to find the red *End* button.

"No! Don't hang up!"

The tone of voice made Colt realize this was serious. "Calm down, brother. What's going on?"

"She's gone. Whitney said three men. I went for a run. Forty-five minutes at the most."

"Slow down." Colt swung his legs out of the bed. "The kids okay?"

"Yeah. Drew slept through the whole thing."

"What about Max? How'd they get past the dog?"

Blake exhaled in a way that almost sounded like a groan. "He was with me."

"And they got past the security system?"

Colt could hear his friend punching something. Hard.

"It was just a quick run on a Saturday morning. I didn't

turn it back on."

"Okay." Colt's head was spinning with the calls he needed to make. "You get the kids somewhere safe. I'll contact the police and get our own team together. Give me a status update in fifteen, and I'll be there as soon as I can."

"Hold on a sec." He heard Blake's breath intensify as if he were walking. "Max seems to have a scent on the old tractor trail."

"That makes sense." Colt knew that land like the back of his hand. There was only one way in and one way out of the property—the same road Blake would have used for his run. The security gate Blake had passed had not been disarmed since he was on foot. The only other way the men could have come and gone without him seeing them was an overgrown tractor path that led to the next property and then out to the road.

"Send the police to Walnut Bottom Road, near the intersection of Bellview." Blake's voice was calmer now, his military training apparently kicking in. "That had to be their entry point. Put at least two of our guys there, too."

"Got it." Colt talked with the phone wedged between his shoulder and his ear as he took a few hopping steps and pulled on a pair of jeans. "Don't worry, bro. We'll find her."

Grabbing a banana and a bottle of water on the way out the door, Colt jumped into his truck and tried to quell the low roar building in his ears. *There has to be a logical explanation. This is northern Virginia. People don't just disappear out of their beds.*

His heart told him that by the time he arrived at

Hawthorne, the issue would be resolved. Cait would be standing on the porch, scolding her husband for causing such an uproar. But his gut told him this was real. *Take it seriously and get the ball rolling.*

He started with the police, giving them as much information as he could, which wasn't much. In all likelihood, if they had taken the same call from someone they didn't know, they probably wouldn't have responded. But Colt convinced them to send at least four officers, including a detective and a forensics specialist.

With his mind continuing to churn and analyze, Colt knew he'd have to sit down with Blake and make a list of Cait's enemies from her days as an investigative reporter. Exposing crime and corruption in the top levels of government had not made her a favorite among politicians—or any criminals for that matter. But why would they kidnap her? And why now? She'd been out of the business and out of the public eye for more than a year. *Could Mallory be behind this?* Colt discounted the name of Blake's ex-wife almost immediately. She was in prison—thanks in part to an investigation by Cait. But even though she knew the property better than anyone, he doubted she could have pulled this off, even if she'd wanted to.

Knowing Cait's background and the powerful people she had dealt with, Colt took a chance and put in a call to an acquaintance at the FBI, as well. This crime had the markings of a case that could evolve and change quickly. He wanted federal agencies to be ready to move if there was any indication Caitlin had been moved across state lines.

By the time he turned onto the dirt road that would lead

him to Hawthorne, he had lined up a team of more than a dozen Phantom Force Tactical specialists to work with the police, and another dozen friends from federal agencies who'd agreed to help as needed in an unofficial capacity.

Done with his calls, his head was on a swivel as he drove the long, tree-lined lane toward the two-hundred-year-old house of his business partner and best friend, looking for anything out of the ordinary. He still couldn't really believe Cait was missing. From her own home. On a brilliantly sunny Saturday morning.

Colt punched the code into the security gate and watched the arm swing open. As he entered the property, he made another attempt to analyze the situation. *What would they want with Cait?* Who would go to this extreme? Was it for money? Vengeance? How did they get in? He was not only shocked by the audacity of those who had undertaken this crime, but also by the failure of Phantom Force's intelligence and security measures to guard against it.

As he approached the house, his gaze fell upon Blake. Dressed in sweatpants and a tee shirt, he stood on the porch with his hands in his pockets, staring out over the fields. Under different circumstances, his absorbed stance could have been mistaken for calmness, but the steam coming off his body in the cool morning air indicated this was not a man who had been standing still for long.

"They weren't after Cait." Blake walked up to the truck and started talking as soon as Colt opened the door. There was a restless intensity about his speech and his movements, as if he were trying hard to keep anguish from overcoming his self-control.

"Who, then?"

"Me." He cleared his throat so he could finish. "They came for the kids."

Now that he was close enough to see him, Colt could tell for certain that Blake's calm exterior was indeed not as resolute as he'd appeared from a distance. His breath was coming in short, uneven gasps, and the knuckles on his left hand were swollen and bloodied from where he'd punched something. Colt put a hand on Blake's shoulder and saw for the first time the raw agony in his friend's eyes. "The kids taken care of?"

"Yeah." Blake ran his hand through his hair. "I got Maggie to pick them up, and I sent Cory along to keep an eye on her house."

"Good deal." Colt didn't say it, but he was glad Blake had sent security along with the kids. They didn't know what they were up against yet. "Tell me exactly what Whitney said. How many were there? Can she count? Did she know?"

Blake held up three fingers. "She said this many."

"And she never saw them before? She didn't recognize them?"

"She said she couldn't see them."

Colt's face crinkled in confusion until he thought about it from the viewpoint of a four-year-old. "They wore masks."

Blake nodded. "That's what I'm thinking she meant."

"What about gloves? Were they wearing gloves?"

"She said she didn't think so, but I'm not sure she remembered."

"Okay. That's something to go on anyway."

"One more thing," Blake added. "She said they were tan."

"Tan?"

"I think she meant brown."

Colt's mind was turning. That could be important—or not. He stared at the house in silence before speaking again. "So what did she say happened to Cait exactly?"

"She said the man told her to come along with him, but then Cait came out and told Whitney to run and lock the door. The closest door was Drew's, so that's where she went."

"And Drew didn't hear anything?"

"No. Slept through the whole thing."

"Did Whitney know what happened outside the door?"

"She said they tried to get in, but Cait wouldn't let them." A nerve in Blake's cheek twitched and his voice lowered. "She said she thought they sounded mad."

"What does that mean?"

"'They talked funny' is what she said."

"So-o-o, another language? Is that what she means do you think?"

Blake nodded and then cleared his throat. "She said they made Cait be quiet."

Colt didn't say anything, but his heart did a flip in his chest at the look on his friend's face.

"She said they were yelling at her on the steps and then it sounded like they made her go to sleep—that she got quiet real fast."

Colt suppressed the urge to grimace and close his eyes as he envisioned the scene. Whoever had taken Cait had not hesitated to use violence. In his mind's eye, he saw the desperate struggle that had taken place. Cait would have fought hard, but they had been mad. Madder still when they'd realized that both kids were behind a locked door.

And that door was strong. More than a century old, it was made of solid wood. Blake had recently replaced the skeleton key locks on most of the interior doors with new deadbolts. Anyone who had the expertise to undertake a kidnapping such as this would have seen in an instant that going through that door would require extra equipment or explosives—plus a good bit of time. Time they knew they didn't have.

Cait had probably tried to run once she saw Whitney had managed to get to safety. But they had caught her. Whitney said it sounded like they made her go to sleep. What did that mean? Had they knocked her unconscious? Had she fallen? Did they drug her?

Colt could only speculate about what had transpired, but he knew the end result. Instead of taking Blake's children, they had left with his wife.

Colt's gaze drifted to the front door. He walked up the steps of the porch and stared at the solid wooden door, trying to envision the men who had so violently interrupted his best friend's life. Then his head jerked up to the security camera aimed at the front entrance. Blake hadn't locked the door or re-armed the interior security alarm when he'd left for his run, but the camera would still be running.

What Colt saw caused him to reach up and push at the place over his heart as if to put the organ back in his chest. The camera was still intact, but it had a large piece of black tape over the lens. They had known it was there and covered it. The fact that they could just walk through an unlocked front door had made their job that much easier.

This exploit was bold and audacious, but not reckless or rash. It would have taken a lot of reconnaissance, a lot of watching, and a lot of planning to accomplish the deed so quickly and without leaving noticeable evidence. This was a result of intense study by an enemy who had thoroughly analyzed Blake's strengths and weaknesses, his schedule, his family...his life.

One name came to mind, a person with the resources and the rage to do it, but Colt refused to think about that. Whoever had done this wanted to hurt Blake—hurt him badly. Otherwise, they would have just put a bullet through Blake's head while he was on his run.

Colt glanced at his friend and knew he was thinking that exact same thought—and it was evident from the look of pain on his face that he would have preferred that ending to the agony and torture to come.

Colt cleared his throat and forced himself back to the task at hand. *Three tan men who wore masks and "talked funny." Not a lot to go on, but it was a start.*

"Okay, let's huddle in ten."

Chapter 2

Colt knew he had to take charge and get everyone briefed and on the same page. The local police would be the lead agency and decide what they wanted to do with the law enforcement assets, but knowing the rules and bureaucracy involved, their turnaround time would be slow. They would have to undertake a painfully long process to make sure Cait hadn't just run away—or that Blake wasn't involved in her disappearance—and valuable time would be lost.

With its real-world experience in hostage recon and rescue, Phantom Force had no such obstructions to hinder forward progress. Colt had no intention of remaining idle.

With speedy efficiency, one of the men carried two sawhorses from out of a summer kitchen and another found an old door. This makeshift desk was soon covered with maps and drawings of the house and property lines, while men from the different agencies crowded around. The picture they presented as they leaned over the maps and talked among themselves was that of calm chaos and confidence. This was a gathering of the best of the best in law enforcement and former military. There could be no equal to the specialties each brought to the table.

Colt heard a short whistle and looked around for the

source. Blake stood on the porch with his phone to his ear, motioning for Colt to come closer. "Take this down," he whispered, still talking on the phone. Colt pulled out his cell, started a quick message, and typed in the numbers and letters as Blake repeated them from someone on the other end.

"Thanks, buddy. That could be a big help," Blake said into the phone before hanging up. "That's a license plate number. Can you get someone to run it?"

Colt nodded and texted the number to a contact, then looked at Blake curiously.

"That was my neighbor. He thought it was strange to see a car parked out by the road so early so he wrote the license plate down, just in case. When he saw all of the police activity up here, he thought he'd better let me know."

"Could be a lot of help." Colt shifted his gaze to the men gathered for the briefing and then back to Blake. "What are you thinking? Any names coming to mind?"

"Just one." Bake exhaled loudly as if he didn't even want to say the word. "Carlos."

Colt nodded indifferently, but it took everything in him not to react with a look of alarm. That was the name he'd been thinking, and if it were Carlos... He stopped himself. He would not allow himself to go there. Not with Cait involved. He couldn't get this job done and be thinking about what *might* be happening. He cleared this throat and patted Blake on the back. "We'll get her back."

Turning around, Colt put his hand up in the air and motioned for silence to the men leaning over the maps. He had worked with almost all of the officers here over the years, and he had no doubt his reputation was known to the others, as well. He didn't go around name-dropping, but he had friends in high places, and as a retired SEAL and a former member of the world-renowned Blackwatch security detail, he knew how to get things done.

Colt began the meeting by explaining what Blake had told him about the timeline and abduction. Every few minutes, he would look at Blake to see if he had anything to add, but for the most part his friend remained silent, watching the proceedings with a dull, dazed look in his eyes.

About fifteen minutes into the briefing, Colt's cell buzzed. Seeing who it was, he put the phone on speaker to allow the officer on the other end to give an update on the plate he'd run. It was a stolen vehicle already on the BOLO list—and had been spotted in the vicinity of a murder two days earlier in Fairfax County, Virginia.

"The murders have all the markings of a Carraco Cartel hit," the officer said, "so consider your suspects armed and dangerous." Most of the men didn't need the warning—just the mention of the Carraco Cartel was enough to cause a sudden exhalation of air from some of the officers in attendance.

After disconnecting the call, Colt glanced over his shoulder and saw Blake staring blankly into the distance. His jaw was set in its usual determined fashion, but the expression in his eyes was one of pure dread. To see that look on a man so strong, hit Colt like a punch to the gut. He hoped his eyes didn't radiate the same panicked alarm because it was beginning to look like the mastermind behind the kidnapping was indeed the infamous drug kingpin, Carlos Valdez. Everyone who knew the name understood it was going to take a lot of skill, fortitude—and possibly lives—to get Cait back.

Chapter 3

A general buzzing began as the men whispered among themselves about the latest news. There was no way a group of law enforcement personnel would not be aware of the Carraco Cartel, or of its ringleader, Carlos Valdez—otherwise known as *Senor de la Muerte*: Lord of Death.

Carlos was the most powerful drug trafficker on the planet, and easily among the wealthiest men in the world. He was a man who lived in two worlds: One, a lifestyle of glamour and opulence where he was treated like royalty because of his reputation and prestige. The other, a world of murder, violence, rape, and drugs, where no crime was too brutal and no payback too harsh.

Like a celebrity from the pages of a high society magazine, Carlos traveled the world in style, lining the pockets of kings, prime ministers, and politicians as part of his strategy to keep those in high places looking the other way from his unlawful dealings and crimes. Thanks to his vicious tactics and style of retribution, he operated in the United States almost with impunity.

In addition to his violent nature, Carlos was a master of manipulation, who worked with the help of three formidable forces: power, influence, and money. The fact that he had as much of all three as any man in the world made him afraid of no one.

If it really were Carlos behind this abduction, then the job of finding Cait had just gotten considerably more difficult and infinitely more dangerous.

Colt turned to Blake. "What year did you arrest Alberto?"

"It was about two years ago." Blake appeared deep in thought. "Might have been in April."

"Okay, listen up, guys. We're trying to connect the dots here." Colt's voice was loud but calm. "When Blake was a homicide detective, he arrested Carlos's son, Alberto, for murder. Some of you may remember that just before the trial, Alberto committed suicide in his jail cell."

That news caused a buzz of whispers and a general nodding of heads.

Colt ignored the reaction and typed a search into his phone for information. "Okay, so the arrest was actually in May. Doesn't look like there's a link there." He did another search to see if there was any connection. "And the anniversary of the suicide is..." He paused and glanced at his watch, then cleared his throat. "The twentieth of October. So five days from now."

Again the whispering of the men increased. Colt refused to look back at Blake now. Five days. Was that just a coincidence? Or was this Carlos's way of getting revenge for his son's death? If it were, they had five days to track down a woman who was in the hands of a man with limitless money and resources; a man who would go to any lengths to cause pain and fear. And a man who had no qualms whatsoever about killing in the name of revenge—even an innocent woman.

Colt could almost hear the clock ticking in his ear.

"Were there ever any direct threats?"

Blake stepped forward and answered. "Yes. Right after the suicide. We received a number of phone calls at the precinct where I worked. They were never able to be traced."

"That said?"

Colt glanced at Blake to see how he was handling this. He appeared his usual calm, stoic self now as if he had compartmentalized his sense of loss and fear so he could concentrate on how to get his wife back.

"Basically, the caller insisted that Alberto's death was not suicide. Carlos also did a lot of media interviews, claiming that the police murdered his son and made it look like a suicide to cover their tracks." Blake paused before continuing. "In Carlos's mind, that meant just one person was responsible for his son's passing—the arresting officer."

"So you're saying you were mentioned by name, Detective Madison?" One of the police officers in attendance was busy taking notes, but paused long enough to look up.

"Yes, I was mentioned by name." A flare crossed his gaze and vanished quickly. "The caller said Carlos would make me suffer and feel the same pain of loss he did, or something along those lines."

"Keep in mind that as a homicide detective, threats were not uncommon," Colt added. "And Blake wasn't married at the time."

Blake nodded. "We took this one a little more seriously because of Carlos's name and reputation, but since it had never been definitively traced back to him, and nothing more was heard for such a long period, it pretty much fell off the radar." He looked down and shrugged. "That's about all. It didn't make much sense then—and even less today."

Colt knew Blake would have hand-dug a moat around the property with a spoon if he'd thought for one moment the danger to his family was real. And he had no doubt his friend was going to beat himself up about that for a long time to come. This wasn't a situation where Colt could tell him "suck it up and move on." This was going to hurt.

The fact that a typical Saturday morning had been turned upside down made it that much worse, and so much harder to bear. Blake, a security professional, had taken the dog with him for an early morning run and had not turned the security system back on. He was human. He'd become complacent in this remote, idyllic setting, and believed his family was safe from the evils that existed in the outside world.

Those two lapses in judgment—small decisions made before grabbing a quick bit of exercise—had now mushroomed into a life-changing event that would require a lot of luck and more than a little ingenuity to fix. Would the dog or a security alarm have kept this from happening? Colt doubted it. Carlos had spent too much time and money studying the target. Not having to disarm the alarm and dispatch the dog might have saved them some time, but even if they had to overcome them, it would not have stopped them.

But when Colt glanced at Blake and saw the lines of pain and remorse etched on his friend's face, he knew there was no way Blake would ever accept that and stop blaming himself.

"Just a thought here, guys." Colt let his gaze drift around

to all of the men. "Carlos is smart. He's malicious. And he's egotistical. I have a feeling we're going to hear from him."

"What do you mean?" One of the men looked up from a map.

"Carlos has the power, the money, and the means to hire a hitman—hell, he has a whole army of them. It's clear he wants more than just another quick kill. We need to figure out *what* exactly."

"So you already have a theory on what his motive is?"

"Just thinking off the top of my head here," Colt answered. "Carlos has no aversion to murdering someone he sees as an enemy. It's his business. It's nothing to him. If we take those warning phone calls seriously now, it appears he wants to savor the uncertainty and fear he is creating as much as anything else. Plus, he's got an ego and a reputation to defend."

"You think he's toying with us?"

"Could be." Colt stuck his hands in his pockets. "Let's look at the facts. Carlos obviously studied this family's routine and did a shitload of recon to be able to get this close and get out so quickly."

The men nodded.

"We have to assume he knew Blake's routine of going for a run, so it would have been easy to just take Blake out this morning with a shot to the head and be done with it. Right? As isolated as this place is, it would have been quick. Bang. Done." He snapped his fingers.

"He wants Blake to suffer." Podge, a communications and technology wizard for Phantom Force spoke up.

"Exactly. And he wants Blake to know who did it. That's why I think he'll make contact." He nodded toward Podge. "You need to be ready for that possibility."

No one said anything for a few minutes, but it was clear what everyone was thinking. It was not going to be hard to make Blake suffer when his wife was in the hands of a madman. The possibilities were endless and made some of the men squirm. Carlos had a reputation for destroying lives without a second thought and killing without conscience. If this theory were correct, they had better track him down and find Blake's wife, fast.

One of the officers spoke up. "If what you said earlier is true—that he was actually after the kids—what do you think his original intent was?"

"Destroy the company." The words were said in a low, even tone, making everyone turn toward the man who had spoken them. Blake.

"What do you mean?" Colt asked.

"I had a high-level meeting yesterday about a contract. We're getting close to inking a deal."

"Yeah. So? We've inked lots of deals."

"This one is the biggest—both financially and in terms of prestige." Blake rubbed his chin as he talked. "So it could be that Carlos intended to take the kids and leak a story to the media that the head of Phantom Force can't even protect his own family."

Colt nodded with a grim look on his face. That scenario would cause the company's current contracts to dry up, and make the businesses that were close to signing a deal pull away. Phantom Force's reputation as a security firm would be damaged, if not completely destroyed.

"It would be a slow, merciless tailspin as far as the business goes." Colt picked up on Blake's line of reasoning. "And the longer the kids were held, the more media coverage Carlos would get. The press wouldn't ignore or walk away from coverage of an event like that."

"Definitely not," one of the officers said. "They would be staked out for as long as it took for the story to run its course—and Carlos would no doubt manipulate the media with leaks and false leads for weeks, if not months."

Colt's mind raced as he analyzed the information. It was surely no coincidence, as Blake had said, that a huge government contract was on the line—and that agreement just happened to be one that required protective services for diplomats and business leaders in Mexico. The timing of that pact's pending approval could not be discounted. Although the deal was not public information, nothing within the Mexican government was safe from being leaked. With Carlos's high-level contacts and endless reserves of money, it was almost certain he knew what was in the contract before even Phantom Force did.

"So you don't think he's going to kill her?" A man that Colt didn't know but who wore the uniform of a local sheriff's deputy spoke up.

"I didn't say that. I'm saying we might have some time. Carlos will play a cat and mouse game. Toy with us. Drag it out." Colt tried to sound optimistic since Blake was standing right behind him, but the end result was not going to be a pleasant one if they didn't find her. Carlos might start by ruining their business as a way to make Blake feel out of control and vulnerable. But when that was completed, he would concentrate on Cait—and destroy Blake's will to live. Colt glanced over his shoulder at this friend.

If he hadn't done so already.

"How do you know so much about him?" One of the men from a local department seemed completely overwhelmed with what they faced.

"I don't know as much as I'd like to, but I did some research a few years back for a government agency." That's all Colt needed to say. Most everyone knew he was a former Navy SEAL, who was now an undercover operative, frequently asked to work on the fringes with covert agencies but not part of the actual fabric of any of them. He no longer served on the front lines of a tangible war. He served at the front of a line that no one knew existed.

As a result, he had a vastly networked web of contacts, including those in the very highest offices of the government. Even though he'd been heavily recruited and personally asked to serve in a prestigious role by the current President of the United States, he'd chosen instead to take his chances on the business he'd started with Blake—the one that was on the verge of being taken down by a Mexican drug lord.

Loyalty. Integrity. Intelligence. Colt was a man everyone wanted to work with on a team everyone wanted to be on. But he knew this case was going to test him in ways he could never have imagined.

Colt's mind kept churning as he turned back to Blake.

"You keep a file on the threats you received?"

"Yes. Should still be on my computer."

"We'll need that to see if there's anything more detailed in those, or facts you don't remember." Colt moved straight into operations mode. "Trin, I need you to work with the police on creating a profile. Share what you find with them and take what they have. Find everything you can on this bastard." He tapped some notes into his phone. "I want an update in thirty."

Trin took the tight deadline in stride, nodded, and walked away to get to work.

Colt turned back to the men and spoke in a voice that did not need volume to get their attention. "Okay, listen up, Phantom Force guys. There's already a BOLO for the car. I want to see the three most obvious routes to Mexico, and I want three teams of two to hit the road—with Tyke and me being one of them. Wheels up in twenty. Gear check in ten."

His voice remained steady and even as more orders rolled off his tongue. "Shirk, I want you and Denton to get a team to check the air, including private airstrips. Podge, you start setting up a Tactical Operations Center at the south end of the house. Let's go."

Chapter 4

The end of the briefing created a flurry of activity. Everybody scattered, heads down, minds concentrating on the specific task they'd been assigned. Huddled in separate corners of the yard, teams got together to plan their parts. The storage room behind the house was unlocked as personal gear was donned and sorted, and equipment divided and organized.

Colt stayed with the group of men from other agencies that now included a task force of unofficial representatives from the DEA and ATF. "The TOC will be in the side addition of the house." He nodded toward the entrance, separate from the main house, which had apparently not been used in the commission of the crime. "If you have any questions about anything, talk to Podge. He'll either answer it or find someone who will."

There was a general nodding of heads.

"Anything we find is yours. We'll pass it on. Hope you'll do the same."

Again the men nodded in agreement as they began making preparations to get down to business.

"One more thing, guys." He didn't raise his voice, but his eyes demanded attention, causing them to grow quiet.

"Carlos has the resources, the rage, and the reputation to

carry this thing off." He paused a moment before making his point. "This is a man who will sacrifice everything to strike a devastating blow against Blake. Every man here has to be willing to do no less."

"We're on the same page," one of the men said as the others nodded in agreement.

"Let's get to work." Colt turned around and almost ran into Jake Brody, one of the Phantom Force team members assisting the police with gathering evidence inside the house. "Can I talk to you a minute, boss?"

"Sure." Colt could see by the look in Brody's eyes that it was important—and that it wasn't good news.

"What's up?" He waited until they were around the corner of the house and out of earshot of the others.

Brody cleared his throat nervously. "Did Blake say anything to you about a pregnancy test?"

Colt could do nothing but stare at Brody as his mind tried to process what he'd just been asked. "No-o-o. Why?"

Brody exhaled through clenched teeth as if he'd been holding his breath, hoping for a different answer. "There was one in the master bathroom. Sitting on the vanity."

Now it was Colt's turn to exhale. He closed his eyes and pictured the scene. Blake had left for a run, and a short time later, Cait had gotten up to take the pregnancy test. The bathroom was closer to Whitney's room than the bed. That's why she'd heard the commotion.

When Colt opened his eyes in question, Brody read the look and gave a single nod. They were teammates. No words were needed.

The test was positive.

Colt put his hand on his chest and rubbed it, surprised at the sudden ache. It felt like someone had just punched him and left him bruised—inducing a pain so acute it took his breath away. He had thought things were as bad as they could be, but now the bottom was dropping out. The fact that this news, under any other circumstances, would have brought joy, made it hurt that much more. These were the two people he loved most in the world. He was elated. He was sickened. His mind could barely register the two extremes of emotion. A feeling of joy followed by a sense of horror.

He put his hand on Brody's shoulder and looked him in the eye. "You'll have to tell him."

"Tell him what?" Blake walked up behind him.

Colt's heart lurched in surprise and then his gaze flicked back to Brody. He wanted to say, "Brody will fill you in," and walk away to start loading his truck, but he couldn't do that to either of them. It wouldn't matter how fast and how far he walked, the dreadfulness of the situation wouldn't go away. He couldn't desert Blake and let someone else tell him the news.

His silence agitated Blake, causing him to repeat the question. Louder. "Tell. Him. What?"

For a split second, Colt considered lying—or at least not telling the whole truth—but he couldn't do either one. It was clear Blake had already sensed that things had gone from bad to worse.

Do your duty even when it's easier not to. The voice of Colt's grandfather whispered in his ear, much as he tried not to hear it, followed by the voice of Blake, who had been the one to deliver devastating news to Colt some years back. Now he knew just how hard that job had been.

"I'll take care of this, Brody." Colt decided to fall on the sword and let Brody off the hook.

Brody almost ran from the scene, but not before shooting Colt an I-owe-you-one look. "Okay, boss."

Colt threw his hand over Blake's shoulder and guided him farther away from the hustle and bustle of the investigation. When they got to the far corner of the house, they stopped, but Colt still hadn't figured out what he was going to say. Even though this was not the first time he'd had to deliver bad news during his career, the look on Blake's face caused his confidence to falter. He'd rather be caught in the middle of an ambush with a limited supply of ammunition than have the duty before him now.

But failure to complete this mission was not an option. He spoke loudly but used a purposeful calming tone. "Not sure how to tell you this, brother."

"Just spit it out, Colt."

"Okay. Here's the deal." Colt drew upon all his strength to look his friend in the eye, but it occurred to him that the tight bond he shared with this man left few people on the planet worse equipped to deal with this situation than he was.

"Brody was sweeping the bedroom for forensics and found a pregnancy test on the master bath vanity."

He let the statement hang in the air a moment, gave Blake a minute to grasp what he'd said, and then nodded, providing an answer to the question Blake didn't have to ask.

A weaker man may have fallen to his knees, or at least showed a sign of the anguish and distress the news had caused. Blake didn't react other than to press his lips closer together and stare out over Colt's shoulder with a look of disbelief, quickly followed by a mixture of sadness, longing, and pain. Colt gave him a few more seconds to absorb the information and then pushed on.

"So, when we get her back, you two will have something to celebrate." He stopped short of saying congratulations. There was too much to lose.

"Thanks for letting me know." Blake put his hand on Colt's shoulder and squeezed, his eyes filled with an unnamed emotion. "I'd rather hear it from you." He turned away and started toward the house, but glanced back once more with a look so full of distress and raw agony that Colt had to put a hand on his chest again. His constricted heart felt like it had just burst wide open.

Blake had survived injuries during the war that would have killed an ordinary man, but Colt knew this hit was worse than any physical pain he'd ever endured. This was a deep wound that affected the soul, and whether or not he would ever re-cover depended on what happened in the next few days—or mere hours.

Colt winced when he heard the back screen door slam closed, but remained frozen where he stood. Ten minutes earlier, he hadn't thought it could get any worse. Now, there were two precious lives at stake—not one—and a man whose entire world was collapsing around him.

Whether or not Cait had seen the positive result was un-clear. But the fact that Blake's unborn child had indirectly saved the lives of his other two children was not.

Chapter 5

Colt didn't have time to complete a pre-combat mission check of night vision goggles, lasers, and radios, but loaded them into his truck anyway. He'd just gotten things in order, and leaned with his arms on the truck bed trying to think of anything he'd missed. Actually, he was stalling. He knew he needed to go find Blake and see if he could provide any words of comfort before he hit the road. But what would he say? What *could* he say?

Just as he decided it was now or never, a duffel bag sailed into his peripheral vision from over his shoulder and landed in the truck with a loud thud. He turned around to find Blake dressed in cargo pants and a tee shirt, fully loaded down with gear, carrying a modified M-4 in one hand, and two more bags in the other.

"What are you doing?" Colt stepped in front of him, blocking his way to the truck.

Blake sidestepped him without stopping and loaded the bags into the bed. "I'm your shotgun rider."

"Negative. Tyke is my shotgun."

"I reassigned him."

Colt's hands curled into fists, but he managed to control his usually volatile temper. The two of them were equals in the company, but not on a mission. Blake had just countermanded one of his orders and put each of them—and Tyke—in an awkward position. Both of them could not be in charge, especially not against someone like Carlos.

Weighing his options, Colt tried to decide how best to handle this unusual and uncomfortable situation. The last thing he wanted to do was upset Blake or give him any more reason to feel helpless. The man had enough to endure without his best friend pulling rank on him. Colt needed to walk the fine line of being a leader without being an obnoxious ass. Even though sensitivity and diplomacy had never been his strongpoints, he gave it a shot. Instead of erupting and issuing a direct order, Colt tried to sound conciliatory by making a suggestion. "Don't you think you should stay here?"

"Tyke can stay. It's going to be dangerous, and he has a wife and a kid on the way."

Colt successfully stopped the reply that was on the tip of his tongue. *So do you.*

"I need you to handle communications on this end. Keep things running smoothly here at the command post."

Blake was not swayed. He continued tying down his equipment. "Podge can do that. Communications. That's his thing." He pointed to the bulge of a phone in the pocket on his leg. "And I have this piece of new technology I can use on the road."

Colt did not smile at the sarcastic remark. Instead, he grabbed his friend by the shoulder just as Blake opened the driver's side door to stow his gun behind the seat.

"Your *orders* are to stay here."

Blake shrugged him off and continued arranging his gear.

"Who do I talk to, to get those orders changed?"

"Me."

"I just talked to you. So-o, it's changed." Blake leaned into the truck and secured his rifle on the floor.

Colt clenched his fists but, once again he successfully checked his temper. "Negative. I'm the lead on this little outing, and *Tyke* is riding with me."

"Wrong." Blake swung around to face him, his brilliant blue eyes smoldering. "Carlos is *mine*."

The words were said with such calculating coldness that Colt knew he had no other option but to react with force now. He pushed Blake against the truck and held him there by his shirt, talking with his face just inches away from his friend's. "This is a police case. Soon to be a federal case if they cross state lines. We're just going to help track them down. We're backup, dude. *Just* backup."

"Carlos. Is. *Mine*." Blake repeated the words as if he hadn't heard a word that had been said. The eyes that stared straight into Colt's were cold and eerily unemotional.

"Break it up, you two." One of the men from a supporting force stepped between them.

When Colt released the tight grip he had on Blake's shirt, the officer began conversing as if nothing unusual had transpired, and in reality, nothing had. Tempers always flared when Type A personalities were keyed up and on edge. In this kind of situation, spats were to be expected.

"Just wanted to let you know there was nothing on either of the cameras," the man said to Colt. "They're taking a closer look in slow motion, but it looks like whoever put tape over them, knew what they were doing. It pretty much just goes to black. No image. Not even a hand that I can see."

Colt had expected as much and nodded. "Thanks, man."

As soon as the officer walked away, Colt turned back to Blake. "This is America, dude." He tried to sound calm and unemotional as he picked up the conversation where they had left it. "Even bad guys get a trial."

"Don't fuck with me, Nick." Blake pushed him out of his way with one strong arm and walked to the other side of the truck.

"Whoa. Now I know you're serious." Instead of getting into a fistfight, which is what Colt would have done under ordinary circumstances, he tried to lighten the mood. "Calling me by the name only my mother calls me."

Colt didn't bother to mention that it was probably only the fifth time in the eighteen years he'd known Blake that he'd heard him swear—and the other four times, they'd been under heavy enemy fire with little chance of getting out alive.

"Yeah. I'm serious." Blake climbed into the passenger seat. "Let's go."

Colt considered pulling Blake out of his truck and forcing him to stay, but quickly nixed the thought. Although they were pretty much equal in size and strength, he knew what Blake could do to a man. He'd witnessed the deadly power of his hands on more than one occasion—and that was when passion and vengeance weren't surging through his veins.

Colt then considered a slight variation of that option. Pull him out and give him a manly hug. Tell him, "I feel your pain and I salute your strength—but you need to stay."

No, that wouldn't work either. Blake would probably punch him in the face and take his truck.

Stalling for time as he tied a tarp down on the cargo in the back, Colt pondered a way out of this dilemma. This was a unique situation that required careful reflection. There were lives at stake. Lives that could be affected now and for years to come.

Under normal circumstances, Colt reasoned, Blake would be the greatest asset he had. Calm, observant, and utterly fearless, he was the type of man Colt wanted in a tough fight. On the battlefield, he was a leader, relied upon by superiors and trusted by his men, a rare breed of warrior that would react with composure no matter what kind of shit hit the fan.

But instead of insurgents or terrorists, it was Blake's wife they were looking for. What if things didn't turn out the way they intended? Would it be better for Blake if he were sitting back here at the house, forced to wonder forever if he could have done something to change the outcome? Or should Colt take him along to be on the front lines? Could Blake live with himself for the rest of his life if he was a key part of a failed mission that could conceivably get his wife killed?

Damn this shit of being in charge.

Colt thrived on planning missions in enemy territory and going into hot combat zones, but making judgment calls like this cut him to the bone—especially when they involved the people he loved most in this world. He was entrusted with a role that could have unseen consequences on other people's lives for eternity, a messy situation that made him feel the weight of command like never before.

Blake opened the door and yelled toward the back of the truck. "You're wasting time. Let's go."

Colt shook his head, put the tailgate up, and walked toward the cab. As he gave one last tug on the bungee cord that held the load in place, he paused and observed Blake through the back window. His friend sat ramrod straight in the seat, staring straight ahead, but Colt could see his left leg bouncing with unleashed energy and knew the man's heart had to be bursting.

It was unusual to see such a display. Blake was a calm, methodical type of guy, who always did things by the book and kept everyone else on the straight and narrow. He'd been the guiding force behind a company that now employed more than three hundred paramilitary, Type A personalities, and he somehow managed to keep them all out of trouble. Phantom Force Tactical had earned respect in the industry because Blake Madison was the kind of man who made sure the company's operatives adhered to a strict, personal code of conduct.

Colt climbed into the driver's seat and glanced over at Blake.

This was not that man.

Chapter 6

Caitlin Madison went from complete unconsciousness to total confusion as she listened to a sound, loud but muffled, coming to her in waves. Her head pounded and she felt vaguely nauseous so she kept her eyes closed while trying to clear the fog from her brain. Where was she? Where was Blake?

Seconds passed—or maybe minutes—before she recognized the sound. Snoring. Loud snoring by at least two people.

Hazy memories began to form, and a soft moan escaped as she tried to shift her weight to look around. She was lying on her side, with her hands tied behind her back. Her rib cage felt bruised and battered. Every breath sent throbs of pain through her back and down her arms. Trying to open her eyes, she groaned again at the pain the effort produced.

A voice, a female one, spoke to her, standing close. "*Estas despierto?*"

Cait pretended she did not understand the question, even though she spoke fluent Spanish. She tried instead to focus on the speaker, but her vision was so blurred she could barely make out the face of the woman bending over her. It took her a moment to realize she was seeing clearly out of only one eye. The other was puffy and swollen.

"*Estas despierto?*" the woman repeated. "Are you awake?"

Cait continued to stare at her. The voice was harsh, but she thought she saw a hint of compassion in the brown eyes. Cait stretched out her legs and tried to sit up.

"*No luchan*," the woman said. Then, seeing that Cait continued to fight her restraints, she repeated her words in English. "Do not struggle."

Cait laid back on the bed, exhausted and drained. "Where am I?"

The smell of cigarette smoke and stale beer hit her along with another wave of nausea. Cait watched the woman's gaze shift guardedly to the doorway where a man's form appeared. He wore a dirty white undershirt and was enshrined in a haze of smoke from the cigarette he held in his hand. His hair was disheveled, and his eyes looked tired. "Tell her to shut up." The words were spoken in Spanish and in a tone that could not be ignored.

"No questions." The woman put her hand out to reinforce her words. "Do not ask questions."

Cait could feel the man continue to glare at her, but her eyes roamed her surroundings. It appeared she was in a hotel room. Her gaze fell on the carpet, brown with stains, frayed, and threadbare, and then to the peeling paint on the walls. Finally, she took in the splotches of mildew that marred the ceiling above her while her stomach did flip-flops. This was not the type of hotel room she would ever think of stepping foot in.

Feeling sweaty and sick, she drew her knees up to her chest. "I'm going to be sick," she whispered. Before the woman could react, Cait moved her head to the side of the bed.

She wretched and gagged, but other than some yellow fluid, little came out. Cait's headache redoubled as she moaned in misery.

"What is wrong with her?" the man in the doorway bellowed in Spanish.

Cait tried to swallow, to cool her burning throat, but her mouth was too dry. She ran her tongue over her cracked and swollen lips, but the metallic taste of blood on them caused her to wretch again. Nothing at all came up this time despite her forceful heaving. How could it? She had nothing in her stomach.

"Hacerla callar." Another man, younger, but no less dirty and disheveled, appeared in the doorway. Make her be quiet. His expression was enough to make Cait whimper, stabbing her with a silent threat. He was tall and lanky, with straggly hair down to his shoulders, and dark eyes that appeared full of anger and hate.

The woman leaned toward Cait and appeared ready to speak when a sudden knock caused instant silence in the room.

"Is everything okay?" a young woman's voice asked through the door.

"*Sí. Sí,*" the woman beside the bed answered. "My brother had too much to dreenk."

Caitlin listened to the footsteps fade away.

"Water?" Cait mouthed the word more than spoke it.

"No." The man in the doorway spoke harshly to the woman when she turned to the bathroom. "Carlos *dijo que su sufrir.*"

Carlos said make her suffer? Cait translated his words in her

head as he turned and stormed back into the adjoining room.
Who was Carlos? She closed her eyes and concentrated on
breathing, on anything but the pain and nausea.

Cait dug back in her memory for any recollection of a
Carlos she had covered in a story or run in to while working
as a journalist. Her mind was blank on that account. Instead,
it drifted back to the morning of her abduction. Was that *this*
morning? Or days ago? Had mere hours passed? Or a week?

She turned her head toward the window. The curtains
were closed, but light oozed in from the edges. It was daytime.

But what day?

Closing her eyes so she could concentrate, Caitlin attempted to clear her mind. But the harder she tried to remember how she had gotten here, the more her head throbbed.
She must have groaned because she heard the woman lean
over her.

"Take a deep breath, *señora*."

Caitlin didn't bother to open her eyes but did as she was
instructed. That simple action brought to mind with vivid detail her last conversation with Blake, and that irresistible half-
cocked grin he'd shot her before closing the bedroom door.
Her heart knotted with pain at the thought of it, and a feeling
of love and longing flooded through her so intensely it took
her breath away. Just an ordinary exchange on a typical Saturday morning that left her gasping with the memory of it. She
never dreamed she could love a man so much.

Again, her muddled mind refused to stay focused. Had
that been hours ago…or days?

Was it *still* Saturday?

More pieces of the puzzle started falling into place, but then a sudden wave of nausea hit her, just like it had in her bedroom after Blake had left. That's when she'd gotten up and pulled out the package she'd hidden in the back of a drawer a few days earlier.

Her heart lurched again at the thought. Taking the test had been a step that made it all seem so irrefutable and certain. If the test turned out to be positive, she wasn't sure she was ready.

Was Blake?

How would she tell him? What do you say to a man in his forties who already has two kids and has just started to fulfill a life-long dream of creating a very time-consuming and physically demanding business? This had not been part of their plan for the future.

Caitlin felt her hands begin to tremble behind her as she thought about the emotions that had coursed through her body when she'd placed the strip on the vanity. Excitement. Utter fear. Happiness. Complete panic.

Knowing she'd never get back to sleep, she'd gotten dressed and sat on the side of the bed, staring at her phone, contemplating sending Blake a text message.

Something vague like: *Remind me to tell you something important when you get home.*

Caitlin closed her eyes tighter now at the insanity of it, and at what had happened next.

Before she'd even gotten a chance to check the results of the strip, she'd heard Whitney cry out.

At first, she'd just assumed the youngster was having a

nightmare, but the cries were louder and more desperate than usual. Opening the door, she'd seen a man wearing a mask dragging the struggling child toward the stairs.

That image jolted her back to the present and caused her to forget about everything else. She raised her head and gazed around the hotel room in desperate anguish. *Are the kids safe? Did they get away?*

Her gaze shot up to the woman. "The babies?"

"They are safe," the woman said with a heavy Spanish accent and no sign of compassion now. "*You* are not."

Caitlin let her head fall back down and breathed a sigh of relief, despite the warning tone. She would gladly take the place of two innocent children—even if it meant losing her life at the hands of whoever had kidnapped her.

But oh how she longed for the protectiveness of Blake's strong arms and the feel of his heartbeat against her cheek.

"You have caused much trouble, Mrs. Madison." The woman spoke again.

Caitlin barely heard anything other than *Mrs. Madison.* Blake often called her that—like he enjoyed the sound of it, or maybe, like her, he still didn't quite believe they were married.

Their meeting and their courtship had been anything but typical—but boy had he spoiled her these past months. He was her rock. Her protector. Without him by her side, she wasn't sure she was strong enough to survive an ordeal such as this.

"Trouble?" Caitlin blinked, her mind replaying what the woman had said. "What did I do?"

"Carlos wanted the children."

Caitlin closed her eyes. He wanted the children? Her groggy mind finally shifted to a new direction. Of course. That was why they'd grabbed Whitney. So Blake was the intended target? Not her?

She recalled a little more now. Remembered seeing three men in the hallway. Her eyes darted over to the figure beside the bed. Or was it two men and a woman? They had been dressed in black and had worn masks. It was hard to tell the sex.

At that moment, she made eye contact with the woman beside the bed, who quickly averted her gaze.

More memories formed, coming to her through a dim haze, surreal, bizarre, slightly out of focus. But the simple act of remembering the sound of the deadbolt on Drew's door latching into place after Whitney had run in sent a flood of relief washing over her.

Knowing the kids were safe had sent her scrambling for the stairs right outside Drew's door in a futile act of self-preservation. Half-running, half-falling down the steps, all the while yelling for Whitney to stay behind the locked door, she remembered lunging for the doorknob.

She closed her eyes tighter, tried to see what had happened next, but all she could remember was a hand yanking her by the ankle, and then a blinding pain in the back of her head, causing the scream to die on her lips.

"Who is Carlos?" Her voice cracked from lack of moisture.

"A powerful man, *señora*."

Without thinking, Caitlin felt her back pockets with her fingers, searching for her phone. Surely she had stuck it in there. Her hopes fell when she found nothing. Had she dropped it? Or had they taken it? She tried to remain strong, but the disappointment and despair at not having a way to communicate with her husband was a devastating blow.

"Blake will kill all of you," she said defiantly. Although her husband was loving and gentle as a lamb by nature, she'd heard enough stories about his days as a Navy SEAL to know he could be roused to worse than a lion. A larger-than-life kind of man, he knew how to hunt down and dispatch an enemy—and she knew he would spare no resources to do so.

Her gaze shifted to the woman in time to see a hint of fear replaced by an expression of defiance.

"No. Carlos will kill him."

Closing her eyes, Caitlin did not bother to ask any more questions. They wanted to hurt Blake, and they were going to achieve that by hurting her first. She almost wished she would die quickly in order to rob them of that satisfaction.

Chapter 7

Colt put his truck in gear and pulled his foot off the clutch. "I'm letting you ride shotgun, but I have some rules."

Blake leaned forward, pulled an empty magazine cartridge out of a canvas bag, and began to slide bullets into the slots. "Oh yeah?" His tone was a mixture of sarcasm and anger. "Like what?"

Colt shifted into second, then third, before answering. "For starters, you're not allowed to blame yourself for this."

Blake kind of snorted as he concentrated on his task. "Blame myself? For what? Taking the dog with me—her last line of defense? Or not turning on the security system behind me?" His voice cracked in a way that conveyed deep regret. "Or are you talking about not staying in bed and making love to my wife instead of going for a run in the first place?" He glanced over at Colt. "Because to tell you the truth, that's the one that really gets to me."

Colt took a few breaths before responding so he could be sure to sound calm and in control. But that was easier said than done—the emotional tone of his friend's voice shook him to the core. He knew Blake's despondency was caused as much by the loss of what he had, as it was for what he would have no more. Because no matter how this turned out, the two of them could never go back in time and make this go away. The days of carefree bliss and an isolated sense of security were behind them.

"What I'm talking about is following the rules. If you're not going to stop the blame game shit, you'll have to get out." As Colt slowed the truck at the end of Blake's road, he hit the button to unlock the doors to accentuate his point. "It's your call."

"I'm not going anywhere, and you're wasting time." Blake's voice radiated irritation. "Do you want me to drive?"

Colt shook his head. "No, dude. I don't want you driving my truck." He made an attempt to further console his friend. "Look. Carlos had this shit well planned. They knew everything, right down to where the cameras were. You know damn well what he'd have done to the security alarm and the dog. It wouldn't have stopped him."

He glanced over at Blake to see how he was reacting. "And if it would have gone as planned, it would have been Cait feeling guilty that the kids were snatched while she slept in the next room."

"I wouldn't have blamed her."

"Right. Just like Cait would never blame you."

Blake turned his head and stared out the window. "I don't need excuses."

"It's not an excuse. Just a fact. I need your head in the game, Blake. You'll be dead weight to me otherwise."

"I'm with you, brother. Don't worry about me. Let's do this."

"Yeah. Let's do this." Colt didn't blink. "... As long as you follow rule number two."

"Geezuz. Which is?"

"You've always said trust is the cornerstone of our operation, and faith is how we operate. I'm the lead on this. You take orders from *me*."

Blake's mouth tightened, and his brow creased, but he didn't say anything.

"Is that a yes?"

Colt's phone rang just then, interrupting the conversation.

"Put it on speaker," Blake said.

Colt ignored him as he picked up the phone. Due to the sensitive nature of his business, his phone had specialized capabilities that made it impossible for anyone else to hear the conversation unless it was on speaker. He knew this could be an update from someone, and it might not be something Blake should hear.

It was Tyke. "Guess you heard I got re-assigned."

"Yeah. I heard. But you take orders from me on this from now on. Got it?" He glanced over at Blake, who had apparently figured out who Colt was talking to because he rolled his eyes and turned his head to the window. He still wore an expression of determination and fortitude, but the flicker of pain in his eyes before he looked away was unmistakable. Colt didn't plan on giving any more pep talks or raising the issue about blame again. He knew Blake's sense of loss was beyond words. Nothing he could say was ever going to change that.

"You probably have everybody's info already, but Podge wants me to send you the main police and agency point of contacts that are here." Tyke continued with his briefing.

"That way, you'll have them if we lose comm."

"Thanks, Tyke. Send them to Blake, too."

He moved the phone away and spoke to Blake. "He's sending you all of the POCs.

Colt put the phone back to his ear. "Anything else?"

There was a brief space of silence before Tyke spoke again. "Um, yeah."

Again, a short pause. Colt stared straight ahead, trying to look unconcerned, but the hesitation in Tyke's voice was killing him.

"They found a necklace out by the road on the other side of the property where the car was seen."

"Okay. What'd it look like?"

"Plain gold chain with a single pearl."

"Hold on a sec." He turned to Blake and held the phone against his shirt. "They found a necklace. Chain with a single pearl."

He couldn't quite read the emotions that ran across Blake's face, but the tightening of the jaw and the single nod was enough to tell him it was Caitlin's. A relatively small object that, no doubt, told a big story.

He put the phone back to his ear. "It's hers. Keep me posted." He disconnected the call.

"Where?"

Blake barely gave him time to put the phone back in the charger.

"Out by the road...where the car was seen."

Colt knew Blake was thinking the same thing he was. It could have come off in a struggle when she was being placed into the vehicle—but it wouldn't surprise either of them if Caitlin had ripped it off on purpose to leave as evidence that she'd been there.

"I gave it to her yesterday as an early anniversary present. She still had it on this morning." Blake talked out loud but sounded like he was talking to himself. His earlier anger at the situation had apparently subsided, but he appeared quiet, withdrawn, and worried now. No doubt he was hashing and re-hashing everything he had done on this otherwise normal morning, and kicking himself for not doing it all differently.

"Look, brother. I know this is hard on you, but you got to keep your hopes up. You have a lot to live for."

Blake didn't remove his gaze from the scenery flashing by the window but replied with the calm dispassion of a man who had dwelled long and hard on the same point. "Or not." Then he seemed to pull himself out of the place where his thoughts were going and returned to loading the magazine. "You have plenty of ammo in the back, right?"

Colt turned his head toward him with a look of concern. "Just a reminder. We're not on a seek-and-kill mission."

"Maybe *you're* not." Blake leaned down and pulled out another magazine.

"I'm serious, Blake. This isn't about murder."

"What's your point?" Blake's hands expertly loaded the cartridge as he talked. "I didn't say anything about murder."

"Really? So what would you call it if you shoot down Carlos?"

Blake didn't hesitate. "Justice." He looked over at Colt as if to make sure he'd heard. "I'd call that justice."

"Damn, man. Don't make me regret bringing you along."

"If I remember correctly, you didn't really have a say in the matter."

Colt knew there was no sense in arguing the point. Truthfully, the only way he'd have had a say in the matter was if he'd knocked Blake out cold. The thought had crossed his mind to do so, but he knew he would have had one hell of a fight on his hands in the attempt. He tried to change the subject. "Look, what I said back at the house is true. He doesn't want her dead."

"She's with Carlos." Blake's face was a mass of pain. "Do you think being alive is going to be better than dead?"

"Stop thinking like that," Colt snapped. He felt his own heart ripping in two—he couldn't imagine how Blake was feeling.

"There's no way to sugarcoat this, Colt, so don't even try. It's my wife. It's Carlos."

"They can't be that far ahead of us. They've only had a ninety-minute head start. Carlos doesn't know what he's up against."

Blake didn't respond to that, so Colt tried to think of a conversation he could initiate that would take Blake's thoughts off the situation. But every topic that came to mind led back to Cait, or the kids, or something to do with a happy family. Colt had served side-by-side with this man for more than eighteen years—had known him even longer. They'd drunk together, laughed together, bled together, and almost died together—more than once. They were as close as any two men could be without being related—and yet, Colt had no idea what to say to him. He gazed out the window at the scenery flying by. "This feels just like the good ol' days, doesn't it? You and me and the open road."

Blake looked left and right. "Except for one small thing—there's no one shooting at us."

Colt didn't state the obvious, but he knew they were both thinking the same thing. *Yet.*

Blake leaned his head against the backrest and closed his eyes, pretending to concentrate. "I guess I'm getting old, but I don't remember too much *good* about the old days. Food rotten and scarce. Living conditions foul and overcrowded. Days long and strenuous. Weather, hot as shit or cold as the arctic."

"Exactly." Colt sighed. "Those were the best days of my life."

Blake remained silent as he seemed to think about it. He brought his head back up and nodded. "I guess you're right. Young, fierce, and armed with a cause worth fighting for."

"Damn right." Colt smiled. "We were some bad-ass dudes back in the day."

Blake half smiled for the first time, but it disappeared in an instant, and his expression became serious and thoughtful. "Those days were good, but compared to..." He didn't finish. He just let out his breath and turned his head toward the window, his face branded by a secret pain that looked like it might be there to stay.

Colt knew what he was thinking. Blake's marriage to Cait wasn't an ordinary circumstance of two people falling in love. They were a team, best friends, soulmates. They adored each other, respected one another, and thoroughly enjoyed every minute they spent together. The brotherhood Blake shared with his warrior buddies was special and significant, but it was not comparable to the new life he'd built. It was no longer a matter of before-being-a-SEAL and after-being-a-SEAL. It was before Cait had come into his life—and after.

Colt hoped to God there wouldn't be a new chapter of *before* and *after*.

He tried again to change the subject. "You catch the game last night?" Blake wasn't a super sports fan, but he did like his football. *Maybe I can get him to concentrate on something else for a little while.*

"Some of it. I was finishing up work on that contract."

Looks like I'm on a roll. "You see that touchdown pass? From the forty yard line?"

"Cait told me about it. You know how she is about the Steelers."

Colt's heart sank. *Good job, Nick. Way to take his mind off his wife.*

He should have known Cait was watching. She was fanatical about the Steelers and had jokingly said she wouldn't have married Blake if he hadn't been a football fan—or if he *had been* an Eagles fan.

"She bugged me until I stopped working long enough to watch the replay."

Colt could just imagine the scene. Cait jumping up and down and screaming while Blake had his head bent down over his computer, working on a contract. Thanks to Colt, Blake was probably wishing he had spent those few minutes more judiciously.

"There aren't many women who like watching football as much as Cait," Blake said after a short silence.

Colt nodded. Caitlin was pretty much one-of-a-kind. She had to be to steal the heart of someone like Blake Madison. But Blake wasn't the only one who loved her. All of the guys knew they could talk to her, tease her, and try to match wits with her. She cooked for them, and drank with them, and was always willing to help them. She stole the heart of anyone who met her, yet seemed completely unaware of her natural country girl good looks—the type of beauty that was easy to see and hard to see past.

To Colt, she was part mother figure, part business partner, and part collaborator. In the year since he'd known her, she'd nursed him through hangovers, illnesses, and bad relationships. If she wasn't so head-over-heels in love and devoted to Blake, there wasn't one of the guys who wouldn't have been after her.

Colt had known what it was like to love a woman like that once. He knew they didn't come around twice in one lifetime.

"You okay?"

Colt jerked his attention back to Blake. "Yeah. Why?"

"You looked like you were in a trance. Sorry if this brings back memories of Jen."

"It does." Colt shrugged, even though his friend's ability to read his thoughts was a little unnerving. "But this isn't going to end like that." He looked Blake in the eye. "I won't let it."

Blake nodded. "I imagine she'd be sitting in this seat as your shotgun, not me."

That made Colt crack a smile. "Absolutely. You wouldn't have been able to walk all over her like you did me." He turned his head and stared out the window. "Damn, I miss her."

The undercurrent of shared loss was heavy and clawed through the silence in the truck, a testament to the love and sorrow that linked them together.

Finally, Blake spoke again. "You ever think about falling in love again?"

Colt looked over at him. "Not really. There'll never be another Griff."

Blake half smiled when Colt used the name Jen went by in the military. "You never know if you don't try."

"No, thanks." Colt gazed straight ahead. "I'm a little too busy to worry about stuff like that."

Colt tried to sound indifferent, but wanted to change the subject. He was, for the most part, content being a bachelor. But there were times, like when he saw Blake and Caitlin together, that he longed for a companion and someone to share his life with.

Blake had tried to talk Colt into getting out of this business and settling down any number of times before, but as far as Colt was concerned, a man could overdose on stability and quiet. He didn't want that life. He hungered for pandemonium, chaos, and danger—thrived on it. He couldn't help it. It was in his blood. He wasn't interested in getting tied down with a woman who wanted to tame him—which is pretty much what they all wanted to do.

"The very thing you think you don't want might be exactly what you need," Blake said in a quiet tone.

"Did you just come up with that?" Colt jerked his gaze over in surprise. "That's pretty deep."

"Just something I learned the hard way a little over a year ago." Blake turned his head toward the window again, apparently intent on studying the contrails of airliners in the sky.

Colt knew what he was referring to. Caitlin was something Blake hadn't asked for and didn't want at the time. They'd met at a murder scene when he was a homicide detective and she a reporter. Apparently her dogged determination to find the truth had taken Blake by surprise—or maybe by storm. Colt had heard parts of the story a thousand times, but could only imagine the details.

"Hey, how do we know they aren't in a plane right now flying over our heads?" Blake stared vacantly out the window at the sky. "We could be wasting our time. Carlos has the money for a private jet."

"I got someone at the federal level with their eye on that for me." Colt gave Blake a sideways glance. "A personal favor, not officially."

"What about a private airfield. They're all over the place in this part of Virginia."

"We've got some feelers out on that, too. We can't keep our eye on all of them, but Carlos is trying to outwit us. I think *he* thinks we're going to be looking in the air, so he's got his guys on the road. Just my gut feeling."

"He wants to think he's outsmarting us." Blake seemed to agree. "Hopping in a plane and flying to wherever he is would be too easy. Driving is brazen. Dangerous. He wants to make us look like fools."

"Bottom line, Bolt, he wants you to suffer." Colt hadn't meant to call Blake by his old call sign, but it slipped out. "If they're going by road and we're concentrating on the air..."

"I'll suffer." Blake's left hand curled into a fist as if he had no other way to release the nervous energy that bounded through him. "I hope you're right. I hope we're on the right track so I can take care of this personally."

"Take it easy." Colt glanced over at him. "You haven't forgotten our earlier conversation already, have you?"

"Bullshit," Blake said under his breath.

"For a refresher, I'm the boss." Colt looked both ways before pulling out from a stop sign. "So do what I say and if I want your opinion, I'll give it to you. Okay?"

Blake didn't answer, but Colt could see his lips were pressed together as if he had a comment he was trying to suppress.

"Let's just take it easy and follow the advice of Abraham Lincoln on this."

Blake rolled his eyes and looked over at him. "How in the hell would *you* know what Abraham Lincoln said?"

"I almost majored in history, bro. Didn't I ever tell you that?"

"No. I don't think you ever did. Is that when you *almost* went to college?"

"Yeah. The Navy saved me from that mistake."

Blake leaned forward and turned down the radio. "I know I'll probably regret asking, but what did Lincoln say?"

"Mercy bears richer fruits than strict justice."

"Murderers don't deserve mercy." Blake's tone was cold

and unemotional.

Colt had no response to that; try as he might to think of one. With the radio turned down, the silence in the truck became oppressive. Out of the corner of his eye, Colt saw Blake absently run his finger over the top of his wedding band as he twisted it back and forth. Colt knew his friend was praying frantically and fervently, and that the exchange of his life for hers was the bargain being struck with God.

"We're gonna find her, bro." Colt tried to reassure him.

Blake nodded but turned his head toward the window. He was staring at the horizon, but Colt knew he was not noting the beauty of the mountains clothed in their colorful autumn attire. More than likely, he didn't even see them.

Chapter 8

Jimmy Podge stood in the middle of the cavernous room in Blake's house and stared at the mess he had helped to create. Equipment lay strewn all over the floor as men hunted and distributed what might be needed in the next few days. Pelican cases with weapons were open in one corner, radios on chargers lined another wall next to bags of tools and office supplies.

This room was a modern addition to the main house and had its own entrance and a more contemporary decor than the rest of the historic structure. Since it had not been used in the commission of the crime, it now served as their temporary operations center.

Podge felt right at home here. As the top tech guy at Phantom Force, he had spent many hours in this room both before and after a mission—and had taken credit for being the one to dub it their "official headquarters." No, it didn't have a boardroom table—but it did have a twenty-five-foot wet bar curving across the back wall that was always stocked with twenty or more cases of Coors Light and Stroh's. And the three couches clustered in front of a large-screen television on the far wall made it the perfect place to enjoy a football game.

Now it was going to serve as the nerve center for an operation that would be one of the most important they had ever undertaken. As a life-long technology geek, Podge was glad to be a part of this high-stakes mission. Not only did he have his hands on all the latest gadgets already in use by covert agencies, he had a knack for developing his own cutting edge equipment that put Phantom Force a step ahead of everyone else.

Glancing around, he took a deep breath and tried to organize his thoughts. Other than the cluster of three couches, the room was lightly furnished so the various teams today had ample space to work. In a few hours, they would meet as one to discuss what they knew, and provide the information others needed to know. Then they would exchange ideas, refine their objective, and determine what they needed to do next.

By then, this space would resemble a high-tech command post. Right now, it appeared more like organized chaos as men re-arranged the three couches to make more room for the long folding tables that would hold computers and electronic equipment. The secure bunker that would someday house Podge's computers, toys, gadgets and gear was under construction so he would have to make do here.

Maps of the property and country were already affixed to the walls until Podge could get his network of computers with up-to-date satellite images to take their place. Specialized phones were being installed as well to allow for backup communications if they needed secure lines or everything else failed.

Podge heard voices emanating from the other side of the house, and knew the police were still busy dusting for fingerprints and doing forensics. This side of the house was alive with activity as well. Teams of officers and agents were huddled in separate corners of the room, creating a low hum of activity that sounded a bit like an agitated hive of bees. Some of the men were seated on chairs, while others were on the floor, sorting through intelligence or talking on their cell phones with police and informants all over the country. By the end of the day, the walls would be plastered with hand-written notes on large sheets of butcher paper, detailing the key points of what they had found. From this, they would mold a tactical plan.

At the moment, they didn't know a whole lot about whom they would be operating against or where any operations would take place. But with three teams on separate routes heading south, west, and southwest, everyone assumed more intel would be forthcoming.

Podge turned on the television and adjusted the channel to a cable news station, keeping it turned down low. If anything came across about the kidnapping, he wanted to know about it. Personally, he had little doubt that Carlos would leak something to the media. The profile of his personality point-ed to an egotistical man who not only wanted to cause panic but also wanted everyone to know who was causing it. Podge understood the necessity of being prepared for the chaos that would ensue if—or when—the press jumped on the story.

As he pulled cables to a row of tables along the wall, Podge couldn't help but think about the two men who were now traveling together. Friends, yes. Close as brothers, yes. But boy could they butt heads.

In the teams, Nicholas Colton was known as "Colt" and

Blake Madison was known simply as "Bolt"—as in Thunder-Bolt. Colt and Bolt were like two peas in a pod—daring, fearless, and always operating on one speed: Fast forward. You always knew where you stood with both of them—and you'd better hope it was on their good side.

But in some ways, they were different. Colt was a realist, who would be prepared for any outcome—no matter how bleak. Blake had always been an optimist, who hoped and expected everything to turn out okay—at least, that's how he'd been before he was seriously wounded in Renoviah and then abandoned by his government. Admittedly, he'd grown a good deal more cynical since then, but Caitlin had started to turn that around.

In any case, they were two men nobody in their right mind would want to mess with. Both had that rare mix of courage that struck fear into the hearts of enemies—a desire to live but a willingness to die. Separately, either one was perfectly capable of doing to Carlos what should have been done by the authorities a long time ago. Together, they were an unstoppable lethal force of nature. If Podge had to put money on who was *not* going to survive this ordeal, it would be Carlos.

As Podge crawled under a table to find an electrical outlet, his thoughts drifted to the first time he'd met Colt. It had been at a bar in Virginia Beach after a hard day of training. No one had needed to tell Podge that this was a fellow soldier. One look at him and you could tell he was a warrior.

Tall for a SEAL at about six-two, he had dark hair and penetrating eyes that had the ability to stop a man with a mere look—or attract a woman with a mere wink. But it was his presence, not his physical stature so much, that drew attention. He had a manner about him that telegraphed a total disregard for his own well-being and an intrepidity easily mistaken for ferocity. Danger pretty much radiated from every lean-muscled inch of him.

After working with him on a few operations, Podge had learned that Colt was at his best when shit hit the fan. Calm. Collected. Able to think—or talk—his way out of tight spots. When his comrades came under attack, they could look confidently to him for leadership. And when his enemies tested his resolve, they soon discovered it was firm and unyielding. He was never afraid to take the shot. Never afraid to lead the way.

Yet he had a great sense of humor too, with the uncanny ability to draw pleasure from the deepest shadows and laughter from the darkest moments. As fearsome as his reputation was, his smile would put you at ease.

Podge chuckled to himself. Back in the day, Colt had been hailed as The Imminent Threat Suppressor on his SEAL team—which in military lingo became known simply as their TITS expert. As a bachelor, he laughed at the title when among the men, but woe to anyone who said it in public.

Dammit. Podge rubbed the back of his head after knocking it on the table. Unlike Colt and Blake, he'd put on some weight since leaving the military, and wasn't as agile as he once was. He crawled the rest of the way out and pulled himself onto a chair.

A little knock on the head is nothing compared to what those two are going through.

Everyone knew this was a devastating blow to Blake, but

it had to be hard on Colt, too. It would be impossible for it not to bring back memories of the hostage rescue op that had killed the woman he loved. Even though he was in no way responsible for Jen's death, everyone knew he blamed himself. She'd been a last-minute replacement on the op at his request, but anyone familiar with *Griff* knew she'd have found her way onto that helo with his permission or not. She was as passionate, obstinate, fearless, and tenacious as Colt. They were made for each other.

Podge frowned. Too bad they'd met in a war zone where it was neither permitted nor safe to have a relationship. Neither of them was willing to break the sacred rules of the military or violate the Uniform Code of Military Justice by having an affair—but Podge had often seen them communicate through wordless messages and react as one, almost as if they thought as a single entity. They had been bonded by something no one else was a part of, and few could understand; a connection more intimate than physical contact, beyond the level of words or even thought.

Even though the mission that night had safely extracted fifty foreign hostages, Colt had lost Griff. In Colt's eyes, the success was outweighed by the loss; a fact he would never forgive himself for or get past. He'd left the service shortly after that, but it hadn't taken him long to miss the danger and chaos of the battlefield.

Colt ended up working for private security firms both home and abroad, and was in the right place at the right time to save the life of a senator from his home state of Texas. The senator, a former military man himself, had taken a liking to

Colt and they'd kept in touch over the years.

That senator was now President of the United States.

Colt wasn't one to abuse that friendship, but if push came to shove, everyone knew the tight relationship could help provide access to information and personnel usually off limits—and under the most desperate of situations, could be used to coerce cooperation from others.

"How do you think it's going on the road?"

Podge looked up from the computer he was booting up to see Tagg, a former SEAL sniper and now one of Phantom Force Tactical's best marksmen. A Kentuckian in his thirties, he stood about five feet ten with an enviable farm boy build. His claim to fame was shooting an acorn out of a squirrel's paws with a BB gun...when he was ten.

"I'll take a wild guess and venture to say there's not much conversation."

Both of the men laughed. Neither Colt nor Blake was much for talking. Both were quiet, stoic, some might even say secretive, always keeping their thoughts and feelings to themselves. Colt could be gregarious if necessary for a job, but that was usually just a ploy to get someone to talk before he did them serious harm.

Tagg became solemn. "I hope this turns out okay."

Podge nodded at the possible magnitude of the loss if it didn't. "This is going to test everyone here. We've rescued brothers in war zones before, but this is a tough one."

"Especially for Blake."

"Yeah. I'm surprised Colt let him go along."

"I'm not sure he had a choice," Podge said pensively. He

wasn't sure it was a good thing either, but there was nothing that could be done about it now.

Other men began filing into the room, ending the conversation.

Podge pointed to the coffee pots lined up on the bar. "Fresh coffee, guys. And homemade apple pie."

"You shitting me?" one of the men said.

"No sense in letting it go to waste. Caitlin would want you to enjoy it."

Podge went back to his computer and worked on a staffing schedule to ensure there would be someone awake and on the phone twenty-four-seven. Others would be on call as needed, while still others would work night and day, tracking down everything they could find about possible safe houses or properties used or owned by Carlos.

Only a handful of men on the planet could be successful on a mission as dangerous and large in scope as this, and Podge had most of them in his contact list. The men of Phantom Force were as comfortable conducting tactical reconnaissance on a conventional battlefield as they were infiltrating a foreign capital wearing suits and carrying false passports. What they lacked in numbers against Carlos's army was more than made up for in skill and experience. Their tenacity, when combined with the battlefield experience each man brought to the table, would surely give them an edge—even against an adversary as cunning as Carlos.

Phantom Force's core was made up of a tight-knit group of employees, and they each wanted to make a major impact on the war on terror. But in addition to that, the company had a vast network of operatives all over the country—and the world—from which they could draw to meet a mission's requirements. Blake and Colt's primary objective was to tailor the force to the individual situation and always keep that force small and cross-functional.

"Might have to dig into the big stuff for this one." Tagg unclipped a key from a bulletin board Podge had hung by the door. "You good with that?"

"Yeah. I'm trying to get that all sorted out. You may as well get into the warehouse and start loading. When they call, we need to be able to hit the road running."

Around him, the room buzzed with tapping keyboards, beeping phones, and whispered talk, all blending to create an amplified thrum of background noise that Podge tried to block out as he thought about what they would be up against with Carlos. They needed someone daring, unconventional, and unremitting to lead this thing—and Colt was that man.

"Don't be stingy with the ammo." Podge tried to yell loud enough for Tagg to hear. Turning back to his computer, he said a silent prayer for the ones who were going to need it most.

Blake and Colt were indomitable spirits, men of courage, who would fight only to win. They might be outmanned by this diabolical adversary, but they could never be conquered. *Never.*

Colt and Blake drove for hours with the radio up loud so there was very little talking. As the sun began to sink down below the horizon, Colt pulled onto an exit ramp. "Let's get something to eat. Truck needs gas."

Blake looked like he wanted to argue the point but must have seen something in Colt's expression that stifled further protest. "Okay. Something quick and a bathroom break."

Colt pulled into the first fast-food joint he saw and got out of the truck, his head on its usual swivel as he surveyed their surroundings. "Looks like a pretty laid back place." He tucked some equipment under the tarp. "This stuff should be safe for a few minutes."

To a casual observer, they were just two guys grabbing a quick meal, but anyone taking a closer look would notice the confidence with which they carried themselves and the intensity in their eyes.

These were not ordinary men.

Chapter 9

Caitlin lay on her side on the bed and stared at the window. Even though it felt like a few hours had passed, she could see it was still daylight and knew it had only been minutes. When a shadow fell across her, she instinctively lifted her head and saw the man in the white tank top standing over her with a pair of scissors in his hand.

Cait's gaze darted to the woman, but she could tell by the look in the woman's eyes, and the tone of the man's voice there would be no argument.

"Sentarsea la señora."

Cait pretended not to understand and did not move, so the woman repeated it in English. "Sit up."

The man did not wait for her to obey the command. He dragged her legs to the side of the bed while pulling her upright. Cait grimaced at both the pain the action caused and the smell. Sweat. Smoke. Alcohol. Singularly bad enough, but mixed together, it was almost unbearable. She closed her eyes and tried to keep from vomiting, afraid it would increase his anger.

When he pulled a large clump of her hair to the side, Cait opened her eyes long enough to see his look of grim pleasure. She closed her eyes again, but that did not stop her from hearing the jaws of the scissors close, and then a slight tug as the hair let go. He repeated the maneuver on the other side and then the back.

She felt a push on her shoulder and opened her eyes long enough to see the man holding her long blond locks in front of her. His lips were spread wide with satisfaction, more clearly showing a row of crooked, yellow teeth set between dry, cracked lips. She tried not to give him the satisfaction of a response but had to look away to keep from crying. He read the reaction and laughed before grabbing her head and pushing it between her legs.

Before she could react, Cait felt something wet being squeezed from a bottle onto the hair that remained. "A new look for you, *señora*," he sneered in Spanish.

The smell of the dye and the shock of the deed sent a new wave of nausea through Cait. She struggled to put her head into the nearby garbage can and choked and wretched again.

"*Por que esta ella enferma?*" the man growled. Why is she sick?

The woman shrugged and did not reply but shot Cait a look of sympathy that suggested she understood. "We must wash that out in twenty minutes." She then placed a towel around Cait's head and pushed her back down onto the bed. Cait closed her eyes as the man disappeared again, trying to blot out the memory of the sound of the scissors cutting through her hair. After a length of time, she opened her eyes and made another plea for water, whispering so only the woman could hear. "Water?"

She pretended not to hear.

Cait decided to try a different tactic. "What's your name?"

Again, the woman pretended not to hear, so Cait spoke louder. "What is your name?"

The woman jerked toward her and put a finger to her mouth, her eyes nervously scanning the door to make sure the men did not hear. They had disappeared into the other room, and could be heard shuffling around as if they were getting ready to lie down again.

"Maria," she finally whispered.

"Maria, I need to go to the bathroom."

The woman eyed her suspiciously and then went into the next room and spoke to the men in whispered Spanish. When she returned, she removed the towel and helped Cait to stand, then cut the zip ties from her wrists.

Caitlin rubbed the circulation back into her arms and followed the woman to the bathroom. "Hurry. I give you two minutes. Then we must rinse your hair."

Walking into the bathroom, Caitlin tried not to look at the large mirror over the sink. But what she saw from just the corner of her eye as she walked in made her turn her head more fully. Her hair, still wet and discolored from the dye was chopped unevenly short. That, combined with her swollen eye and pale skin, made her appear like something from a horror movie. She stifled a whimper as she brought her hand to her mouth.

Maria had not closed the door and must have heard her as she waited off to the side. "Hurry, *señora*."

As soon as Caitlin had relieved herself and flushed, she bent over the sink to wash her hands and gulped thirstily from the faucet.

"That's enough." Maria pushed her head under the spout and began to rinse the dye. When she was done, she grabbed a towel and wrapped Caitlin's head so Cait could not see the finished product and tried to hustle her from the room.

Caitlin stopped at the door and planted her feet. "Please. I want to go home."

The woman looked at Cait and then away. "You will not be going home anytime soon."

"When?"

"I do not know. Stop asking questions."

"Why are you doing this? Cait pleaded.

"Not why you think."

"You don't know what I think." Caitlin's voice rose in anger.

"Quiet," the woman hissed, holding her finger to her mouth again. "You must not talk."

Maria led her back to the bed and motioned for her to lie down. "You must be quiet and rest," she whispered.

"Why?" Cait spoke softly. She did not want to wake the sleeping men any more than Maria did, but she wanted to keep Maria's mind occupied, hoping she would forget to bind her hands again. Blake's voice came to her as clearly as if he were standing right beside the bed. *Hope is not a strategy, Cait.*

Caitlin's mind raced. *Dammit. How am I supposed to come up with a strategy? I've never been in this situation before.*

Once she had sat down on the bed, Maria gave her a gentle push to make her lie down. "Rest."

Caitlin nodded and closed her eyes, then concentrated on looking relaxed and breathing slowly. She could tell Maria was standing over her, trying to decide whether or not to restrain her.

"Give me your hands, *señora*."

Caitlin's heart plunged. She held her hands while Maria tightened a zip tie around them. "Now you must rest."

Caitlin did not answer. She turned her head away and closed her eyes as she listened to the sound of Maria sitting on the other bed. At least her hands were tied in front of her now. She could at least be thankful for that.

Trying to appear calm and relaxed was the hardest thing Caitlin had ever done because every nerve was on high alert, trying to figure out a way to escape. She had no idea where she was or how she would get away, but she was not going to sit around and wait to meet the mysterious man named Carlos.

Chapter 10

Caitlin studied the light trickling in through the closed curtains and attempted to guess again how much time had passed since her abduction. Was it still Saturday? It had to be, yet she had no idea how long they had traveled to get here. From the angle of the light streaming into the room, the sun was getting lower in the sky, going down. Yet everyone had gone back to bed. The only thing she heard from the next room was a cacophony of snoring. She turned her head and saw Maria lying on the bed, seeming to be resting as well.

Cait's mind drifted back to Blake and the peaceful, quiet life they had lived at Hawthorne. It was a life she had taken for granted and always assumed she would have. She never dreamed there would be a day when Blake's arms weren't open, waiting for her to be pressed between them.

What is he doing right now? She closed her eyes. Tight. *By now, he knows about the pregnancy test. Did he find it himself? Or did Colt or one of the guys discover it?* She swallowed to keep from gagging at the thought of him hearing such news in such a way.

Even though she'd never seen the result, Caitlin instinctively knew it was positive. Deep down, she'd known before she'd even taken it, but now, with the sickness, she was certain. And there was no denying the protectiveness she felt for the being growing inside of her. It was not just her own survival she was fighting for now.

Poor Blake. She pictured his reaction when he heard the news. Blindsided surely, and under ordinary circumstances, she hoped, excited. The thought that it may have been Colt delivering the news made it only slightly less tormenting. The two of them were closer than most brothers. Practically inseparable. She'd often teased Blake that if she were the jealous type, she'd be resentful of the close relationship they shared.

Under these circumstances, and at this moment, she found only consolation in knowing Blake had Colt by his side.

Please, God, don't let Blake blame himself for this. She closed her eyes tightly at the thought of her husband suffering, worrying about her. He was the type of man who'd do anything to protect his family, even at the risk of his own life. His only fault had been believing that they were isolated enough from the violence of the world to be safe. She had to get away, get back to him, ease his torment.

As she lay on her back with her hands on her stomach, her mind flitted to the future. It surprised her that she was not more fearful and anxious about being pregnant. Somehow, just knowing she was responsible for two lives made her stronger, more determined to escape and survive this ordeal.

Caitlin remained still, listening to her own breathing and that of the others and then turned her head toward the door. As it came into focus, she stared at it hard, as if by doing so she could get it to open. It was a silly thought. She could see it was chained, probably bolted too, but it was only about twenty feet away.

Let the fire inside you burn brighter than the fire around you. Blake had always given her tidbits of wisdom he'd learned on the battlefield. She'd never really thought she would need to use them.

But she knew she had to try to escape.

Sitting up slowly and waiting for the dizziness to clear, she studied Maria, watching for any signs of movement. The woman's chest moved rhythmically up and down as she slept. She must have been exhausted to fall asleep so quickly.

Caitlin slid her feet to the floor and rested her head between her legs a moment to quash the nausea. *Please don't throw up, Caitlin. Not now.*

When the feeling of sickness passed, she raised her head again. The room remained cloaked in silence except for the gentle breathing of Maria and the snoring of the men in the next room. Slowly, she stood, her heart drumming in her chest and pounding in her throat. Just the act of standing upright caused her to inhale and exhale more heavily—a sound that resonated like a freight train in her ears. She did not advance until her breathing was under control, then slid one foot forward just a few inches. She paused before the next step, every nerve on high alert.

Take a step. Listen. Take a step. Repeat.

She tried to time her movements with the snoring in the next room, but it was a slow and torturous journey. With her eyes concentrating on the doorknob, her other senses remained alert and focused on any movement behind her as inch by inch she moved forward.

When just a few feet away, she realized she had not taken

a breath for quite some time. She stopped and sucked in some air, releasing it as quietly as she could—which sounded like a hurricane wind to her.

Slow is fast. Take your time.

Sucking in a few slow, deep breaths before attempting another step, Caitlin tried to calm her nerves and quiet her mind before proceeding. Every inch of her tingled with expectation when she finally moved close enough to touch the knob. With a trembling hand, she slid the old-fashioned chain from its slot, surprised that it made very little noise. Just to be safe, she waited for the span of ten deep breaths before turning her attention to the deadbolt.

Take your time. Nice and easy.

Caitlin glanced over her shoulder at the sleeping Maria before turning the lock as slowly as she could. The resulting *snap* as it unlatched sounded like a thunderclap. She closed her eyes and held her breath as sweat trickled down her temples. Her entire body trembled. She remained frozen in place, listening. She heard the same steady breathing behind her, so she concentrated on getting her breaths back under control.

Inhale. Exhale. Inhale. Exhale.

Opening her eyes, she stared at the door and knew it was time to move. Every second she lingered was another moment lost. She moved her hand down to the doorknob and turned it, thankful the latch made only a soft *click* this time as it released. The roaring in her ears almost made thought impossible, but she was so close to freedom now, nothing could stop her.

Easing the door open, she stifled a whimper of relief as a

flood of light burst into the room. With adrenaline now surging through her veins, she inadvertently pulled even harder, causing the door to whine and squeak in revolt. Cool, fresh air hit her face. The bumper of a car in the parking space outside came into view. Just another few inches and she could step across the threshold—and then she would run. Run for her life.

Sidestepping so she could squeeze through instead of taking the risk of more noise, Caitlin took a few deep breaths. She would need to be ready to bolt as soon as she cleared the door. With her mind completely focused, she put one foot over the threshold, ignoring the sun edging down over the horizon, its soft rays flooding over her like a warm, comforting blanket.

Bending forward at the waist to see which way she should go, she looked to her right and saw nothing but an empty, abandoned-looking building. She could hear the low hum of traffic coming from somewhere, and had just started to turn to her left when she felt the violent grasp of a hand on her shoulder. It clamped onto her like a vice and shook her.

"Carlos will not be happy," the man said in Spanish as he jerked her around to face him. His tone was enough to tell her he was angry, but the rage in his eyes and the iron grip substantiated that fact. She knew she would have fingerprint bruises on her shoulder as a result.

Caitlin could not stop the sob that rose in her throat as the man shoved her roughly back through the doorway she had just stepped through.

There began much shouting and screaming in Spanish as

the man woke up Maria and chastised her for not binding Caitlin's hands behind her. Maria glowered at her, as if she should not have tried something so foolish, and then began throwing things into a bag as they made preparations to leave.

"Where are we going?" Caitlin asked as Maria threw a coat over Caitlin's hands so no one would notice they were bound together.

Maria did not answer, and the man who had discovered her while going out for a smoke reinforced the message by lifting his shirt and showing her the gun that was stuck in his waistband.

Caitlin had no choice but to walk with them.

Chapter 11

After hitting the men's room and grabbing some food, Colt and Blake were soon back on the road. Darkness replaced the daylight, and the seemingly endless road in front of them transformed into a general blur of headlights and taillights.

Colt had given up trying to start a conversation, so both men contented themselves listening to the radio and reflecting on their own thoughts. The silence was interrupted by Colt's phone. It was Podge again.

"Put it on speaker," Blake said as Colt reached down to answer it.

Colt waved for Blake to be quiet.

"Put. It. On. Speaker." Blake was adamant, but Colt just pressed the phone closer to his ear.

"We might have something."

Colt could tell by the tone of Podge's voice it wasn't good news, but he kept his face blank and his tone unemotional. "Like what?"

He heard Podge clearing his throat nervously.

"What's going on?" Blake put his hand on Colt's shoulder and shook him, but Colt silenced him with his finger.

"There was a commotion at a hotel near Staunton. You might be the closest team."

Colt turned his attention to Blake and pointed at the map sprawled across his lap. "Staunton." Then he returned to his conversation. "What kind of commotion?"

"Staunton? That's behind us." Blake grabbed for the phone, but Colt held him off. "Like a good five hours at least. Are you sure? How did we get ahead of them?" The edge in Blake's voice matched the glint of frustration and anguish in his eyes.

Podge continued the conversation. "Well, a hotel maid heard someone...ummm, vomiting."

Colt put the phone to his other ear as if it would help him hear. "And?"

"A woman with a Hispanic accent said it was just a man who had too much to drink, but the maid was suspicious. She said that's not what it sounded like."

"What did it sound like?"

"She said it sounded like a woman."

"That's not much to go on."

"Yeah, well, she didn't think so either until she saw them packing up and heading out, so she went ahead and cleaned the room."

Colt concentrated on breathing normally. "And?"

"When she was dumping the trash, a bag fell out." There was a long pause. "Full of blonde hair."

Colt exhaled. "I see."

"What do you see?" Blake demanded.

Colt ignored him. "So they got a room this morning and hightailed it out of there at dark. Is that right?"

"Yeah. And something else."

Colt's heart dropped at the tone of his voice.

"The police found the car with that license plate you tracked about seventy miles from the house." Podge paused a moment. "It was up in Pennsylvania, so they must have dumped it up there and then headed south to throw us off track."

Colt's heart sank. Even though it wasn't unexpected, the vehicle's plate had been the only real lead they had.

"Anything of relevance there?" He tried to sound vague since he knew Blake was listening to every word. What he really wanted to know was if there were any obvious signs in the car that Caitlin was injured—or dead.

"Police are doing forensics now. I'll let you know as soon as I hear anything."

The line went silent a moment as if it took a bit for Podge to understand what Colt had wanted to know. "Nothing obvious to the eye. No blood."

Blake saw the look of relief and grabbed Colt's shoulder again. "What's he saying?"

Colt held one finger up in the air for Blake to wait. "Okay, buddy. Thanks for the update."

"One other thing—there isn't much as far as security camera images at the hotel, but we're looking. If we find anything, I'll let you know."

"Good deal," Colt said. "You have locals working on the roads around the hotel, right?"

"Ten-four. State and regional police are on the lookout and actively patrolling." He paused a moment and Colt could hear him tapping away on a keyboard.

"I'm sending you and Blake the latest background info we have on Carlos. Nothing real significant."

"Copy that. Thanks."

As soon as Colt hung up, Blake was leaning toward him. "What'd he say?"

"Good news and bad news." Colt pretended to be leveling with him. "The bad news is they found the car, so they've switched vehicles."

"*Damn.*" Blake ran a hand through his hair. "It was already like trying to find a needle in a haystack. Now we don't even know what the needle looks like." He turned his head toward him and grilled him with his eyes. "What's the good news?"

"A hotel worker noticed something suspicious."

Blake's brow wrinkled as if he didn't think that was particularly good news. "Suspicious. Like what?"

Colt knew Blake wouldn't let him off the hook easily. His mind raced about how much to tell his friend. He decided to leave out the part about the vomiting and the hair. Those two images were not what Blake needed right now."

"Nothing real concrete. But the people in the room were Hispanic. They checked in this morning and checked out at dusk."

Blake seemed to accept that as being pretty suspicious. "So they're going to hole up during daylight hours and drive only at night."

"At least, for today. They probably think we're ahead of them and won't backtrack, so it makes sense."

They were both silent for a moment.

"And it looks like we picked the right route. Podge said

we're the closest team, but since we're ahead of them now, we may as well catch some sleep."

"He didn't say that." Blake leaned back in his seat and rubbed his temples as if he had a killer headache.

Colt could sense the barely controlled energy coiled in his body, and knew that sleep was the last thing he wanted to do.

"You're not telling me everything."

"You're right, he told me one other thing. He's sending us both the latest on Carlos's background."

Just then, both phones dinged with an incoming email.

"Pull it up and give me a summary," Colt said. "I want to see if there's anything new."

Blake opened the email and began reading, to himself at first, but when he got to parts of interest, he read out loud. "His grandfather was born in west Texas, one of twenty-four children, all but ten of which died from diseases or hunger. His father worked in the mercury mines and then squatted on a ranch in the desert that was largely ignored due to its remoteness. Blah, blah, blah. You knew all that, right?"

Colt nodded. "Do we know where the ranch is?"

"I don't see it in this report. I'll text Podge."

"What else does it say?"

Blake studied the email. "His profile says he has a chip on his shoulder because he was always treated like a third-class citizen, even though he is American by birth."

"I guess that gives us a little insight."

"During prohibition, his father bought jugs of cactus moonshine from bootleggers in the mountains and smuggled them into the United States. Says here, smuggling was a way of life—contraband of one kind or another, smuggled in one direction or another, over several generations."

"That's a nice family background picture." Colt tried to lighten the mood. "A chip off the old block."

Blake grew quiet but then began reading again. "He takes obvious pleasure in trafficking drugs and sex in the United States, but he has global ambitions, as well." His voice grew husky, and he read slower, as if he were not only absorbing the words but creating mental images, as well. "He has a strict enforcement policy, which means killing delinquent customers as well as nefarious employees."

"That's enough. I get the picture." Colt regretted asking Blake to open the email.

"I'm almost done." Blake cleared his throat, swallowed hard, and continued.

"Even his killings are carried out in a distinctive manner, mostly as a way to intimidate, so they can be used as an example to others. He is regarded as a vicious and extremely dangerous person, who possesses little regard for human life."

Blake lowered his phone a moment and stared out over the dashboard, his face stamped with pain.

Nice job, Nick.

He should have known a report on Carlos would not contain anything pleasant. It was too late now to try and offer calming words, like "don't worry, everything will be okay." They both knew that wasn't the case.

Carlos was hell-bent on vengeance against Blake…against the United States…and against anything he perceived as standing in his way. Caitlin was nothing more than an insignificant pawn in a large-scale game Carlos was playing.

"He doesn't know who he's up against," Colt said. "You know we got the best guys in the world on this. The tables are going to turn on him."

Colt watched as Blake successfully fought down the panic and returned to the iron calm for which he was so well known. After clearing his throat, Blake brought the phone up and paged down past the part he had just read.

Blake's mouth moved as he read to himself before finding something to share. "In addition to drugs, his business empire now ranges from software piracy and extortion to money laundering and prostitution."

Colt's fingers tightened around the steering wheel. The drug kingpin wanted to hurt and destroy Blake Madison inch by inch. Seeing the pain etched on his friend's face right now, Colt worried that he might achieve his goal. Unlike facing an enemy in a fair fight, this was a battle with no front lines and no end in sight. This information on Carlos's background had only reinforced what he knew they needed to do: Find Caitlin—and soon.

Chapter 12

Caitlin walked between the two men, with Maria following along behind. Part of her wanted to curl up into a ball and cry, and part of her wanted to scream and create a scene so someone would help her. The men on each side of her, bristling with violence, were the only things stopping her from doing the former. And the only thing stopping her from doing the latter was the life inside her she wanted to protect. She would have taken her chances with the men with the knives and guns. But she couldn't do that and risk losing her baby.

Instead, she concentrated on her surroundings. She saw mountains. They looked like the Blue Ridge in Virginia. So maybe it *was* still Saturday? One of the men noticed her looking around and squeezed her arm tighter. When they rounded the corner, they walked toward a maroon-colored minivan that was backed into the parking space. Caitlin's eyes fell on the license plate. New Mexico. Before she could read the number, the men jerked her around to the side. But she caught a glimpse of the last three letters before she was shoved through the open door and into a seat. D-A-V.

Caitlin sat in the back seat while Maria arranged things behind her. She remained passive and quiet, all the while taking in everything—the surroundings, the vehicle she was getting into, and the descriptions of her captors, impressing them all in her memory.

The man Maria had called Pedro, had graying hair, short, thick legs, and a wide middle. He appeared angry all the time—and mean. The younger man, Juan, was taller and lean with jet-black hair. His eyes were shifty and nervous—not malicious, exactly, but obviously fearful enough of his boss to make him capable of performing whatever task was asked of him.

When Maria buckled herself into the seat in front of her, Caitlin leaned forward. "What day is it?"

"I don't know."

"Where are we?"

"I'm not sure."

"Where are going?"

"Stop asking questions, *señora.*"

The men stood outside, talking loudly and smoking. "Is that your brother?" Caitlin nodded toward the older man, Pedro.

"No." Maria sounded angry. "Of course, he is not my brother."

"But that's what you told the maid in the room. You told her your brother was sick."

The conversation ended because the men suddenly threw their cigarettes down and hopped into the van, the older one getting into the driver's seat. "No talking," he spat in Spanish, turning around and wagging his finger at Maria, who appeared scared and intimidated. She shot Caitlin a glance that pleaded for her to be quiet.

Caitlin turned her attention to the window and soon felt a towel being placed over her head so she could not see. Even though every muscle in her body ached, she felt her eyes grow heavy with exhaustion. Perhaps she should sleep now when there was no chance of escape and nothing to see. She needed to be wide awake and rested when the chance did present itself.

As the minivan picked up speed, Caitlin's head began swaying. Maria pushed her down so she could lie across the seat and placed a rolled-up towel under her head. Caitlin wasn't sure if she was being nice or wanted her hidden from view, but her eyes were so heavy, she didn't care. Soon after her head hit the towel, a blanket was draped across her.

Caitlin fell into a deep sleep but was awakened by the sound of a cell phone ringing and Pedro yelling for everyone to be quiet. He turned around in the seat and said, "*Gran jefe*," to Maria before picking up the phone.

Big boss. Caitlin tried to keep her breathing even in case Maria was watching. So the mysterious Carlos was on the phone.

"*Hola*, Carlos."

Caitlin could not make out any words that were spoken on the other side, but she could hear the tone—the violence—through the connection, and that it was a man speaking Spanish.

Pedro answered in Spanish, as well; telling him the package was on its way.

It took her only a moment to realize they were talking about her. *On its way to where?*

More chatter from the other end of the line, and then laughter as Pedro spoke in Spanish so fast she could barely translate in her head. "A great plan, Carlos. They will not venture to Mexico. The package will be safe with you there."

Caitlin tried to keep from groaning out loud. *No. Not Mexico!* Even though Blake's friend Colt knew the President personally, the international ramifications would hinder any chance of rescue. It would take time to get authorization to launch a raid on foreign soil—not that Colt or Blake would necessarily wait for permission. Still, she needed to do everything in her power to take things into her own hands...to get away while she was still in the United States.

She swallowed the lump in her throat and tried to strengthen her resolve. She knew what it would mean if they successfully transported her across the border. She'd read the headlines: Vicious wars being fought between rival factions over control of drug profits. Innocent people dying in the crossfire. Even policemen—both innocent and corrupt— were being slain or forced to flee for their lives. And there would be no help coming from local, state, or federal police, most of whom were involved in organized crime.

Blinking hard against the onslaught of tears, she strengthened her resolve. It just meant she had to try to escape before they reached the border. They had to be days away.

The next bit of conversation confirmed that. Pedro told Carlos they were almost into Tennessee, and would make it to Texas the next day. No matter where they were heading from there, it would take at least another day of travel to make it to the Mexican border. She had a little time.

Caitlin allowed her mind to wander to Blake. What was he doing at this very minute? She could only imagine the pain he was in, worrying about her, blaming himself. Her stomach began to churn at her desolate thoughts. She ran her tongue over her dry lips, trying to think of something else, but the wave of nausea just grew stronger. She shifted her weight to reposition herself to help relieve her cramps.

"Are you going to be sick, *señora*?"

Maria removed the towel and leaned over to look at her more closely.

Caitlin nodded just as she began to gag and wretch into a plastic bag held out by Maria.

She heard Pedro say a hurried *adios* to Carlos before he started screaming at her in Spanish.

"She cannot help it." Maria's voice rose to the same level as his, which silenced him. "All of the drug money in the world cannot stop it."

Caitlin was exhausted, but that wasn't what caused the spinning, out of control feeling that had just enveloped her. *Drug money? Carlos?*

The pieces of the puzzle started to come together, but Caitlin almost wished she were still in the dark about it. Carlos Valdez? Anyone who knew anything about current events knew the name—and knowing the name was enough to send shivers down anyone's spine. He was known mostly as the world's richest drug kingpin, but having read stories about his exploits, Caitlin had other ways to describe him. Malicious. Vicious. Violent. Vindictive.

She remembered reading about the arrest of his son a few

years ago, and the son's subsequent suicide in jail. She had not covered the story when she was a newspaper reporter—only read about it. Why would he be targeting *her*?

Blake. He'd been the arresting officer. Her husband had never spoken about it directly, but she knew that it had been one of the biggest cases he had ever been a part of.

Cold fingers of despair started working their way up her spine. She knew how these kingpins operated, and knew that Carlos was among the wealthiest and most powerful of them all. He could put contracts on anyone he knew or suspected was interfering with business—including politicians and those in law enforcement. And in this economically depressed area, it wasn't hard to find someone who would do the deed in order to get on his payroll.

She tried to control the river of negative thoughts. She had to keep her wits about her. Be alert at all times. Be ready to run when the chance presented itself.

Blake was on the trail. She knew he was—perhaps was even watching them right now. And there would be no limit to the pain he would inflict. She felt a sense of calm wash over her and then realized the vehicle was slowing. Perhaps they needed gas. Now might be her chance to escape.

Caitlin felt the van come to a stop and looked up to see the lights of urban sprawl flooding down from above. She noticed that Pedro now wore a ball cap pulled down low over his face, while Juan wore one backwards.

"Are you hungry, *señora?*"

Caitlin didn't know if Maria was being serious or joking. She had not eaten anything more than the banana Maria had given her at the hotel room. Yet the smell coming from the restaurant was causing her stomach to do somersaults again.

But she didn't care how weak she felt. If a chance to run presented itself, she was going to take it.

She soon found that easier said than done, however. Now that she had tried to get away once, none of them trusted her. Once they stopped, Pedro went in to order the food while Juan went to the restroom. Maria and Caitlin went to the bathroom too, but Maria waited right outside her stall until she was finished, then escorted her out to the van once more to be watched by Juan.

Caitlin looked around, trying to catch someone's eye—anyone—but no one was paying attention to anything other than what was in his or her own little world. There were mothers with children, teenagers hanging out, and a few couples sitting at tables eating their food. No one even seemed to notice her except for an older man sitting by himself at the window—and that was only a curious glance. With the way she looked, she couldn't really blame him.

Caitlin sat in the van with Juan, while Maria went back inside to use the restroom herself. The young man made her nervous. He'd turn around and stare at her every few minutes, most likely to make sure she wasn't thinking of trying to run. Caitlin's heart sank when she realized how closely she was being watched. It was like observing a game of musical chairs. There wasn't a moment when someone's eyes weren't on her, and their intense looks made her realize they had permission to do whatever it took to stop her from getting away. She began to lose hope.

Chapter 13

"You've got to be kidding me." Blake glowered at Colt as he pulled into the parking lot of a hotel. A garish light flashed *Vacancy* over the office door, except the second 'c' wasn't lit so it read *Vacany*.

"Do you have a special app on your phone that finds hooker hotels or what?"

"Hey, I'm a bachelor. I have intuitive radar for cheap hotels. I don't need fancy sheets like you do."

For just a second, Colt thought he saw the glimmer of a smile on Blake's face at the comment, but it quickly transformed itself into something that more closely resembled a scowl. Everyone close to Blake knew that marriage had ruined his ability to sleep on a dirty bedspread or a stinky couch. This was a man who had once seemed perfectly comfortable catching Zs on a slab of concrete, or a patch of mud, or curled up in a ditch in a sandstorm—but the act of getting hitched had changed all that. Caitlin was not a prissy, girly type by any means—but she 'had a thing' about staying in anything less than a four-star hotel. In a year's time, Blake had somehow acquired the same inclination.

Blake bounced his head off the headrest behind him a couple of times. "What are we doing?"

"I'm going to get some sleep. I'd advise you to do the same." Colt leaned over and grabbed his wallet from the center console. "I'll even buy. You're good with sharing a room, right?"

Blake stared straight ahead. "I'm really not tired."

Colt ignored him. "I'll spring for two beds, so don't even think about spooning with me like you did in Afghanistan."

The comment did not elicit a smile, but it did cause a snort.

Colt got out and then leaned back in to squeeze Blake's arm. "You gotta get some rest, dude. A couple hours. It might be the last time we stop for days. You need to shut it down."

Blake inhaled but didn't let it out right away. "Okay, Mommy. You win."

While Colt checked in, Blake secured some of their gear in the locked cab and loaded up with the most valuable equipment to take into the room. "I'm guessing there's no room service," he said when Colt unlocked the door. It creaked open to reveal two lumpy-looking beds and a television set that had seen better days. One of the ceiling tiles was missing, and the others looked ready to fall at any moment.

"There's a fast food place right across the parking lot." Colt reached down and turned on the light while looking hesitantly around the room. It *was* pretty bad—even by his low standards. "That'll do, right?" He threw his bag on one of the beds.

"Sounds great." Blake's lips were pressed together as if getting ready to endure a secret torture. "Can hardly wait."

"I promise, it will be better than MREs."

"Now that's going out on a limb." Blake said the words while standing with his hands on his hips, staring blankly at the television as if he were watching something.

"Dude, you need to turn it on to see a picture." Colt picked up the control and hit the power button. "See? Magic."

Blake continued to stare at the screen, but Colt could tell he wasn't really watching. "So nothing's hit the news yet. Right?" he finally asked.

"No word on that." Colt pulled out his wallet and thumbed through his bills. "Why don't you hit the shower while I run for the food?"

Blake slowly turned his head toward him. "Why don't you just level with me and tell me you want to make some calls without me being around?"

Colt didn't look at the cool, steady gaze of his friend. Those deep blue eyes could be intimidating, and he didn't like lying. "I *was* leveling with you—and trying to be nice. You need a shower a lot worse than I do. Trust me on that."

Blake was sitting on the edge of the bed with his phone in his hand when he heard the door slam closed. Knowing he didn't have much time, he pushed the button to call the kids.

"Just checking in on the little monsters," he said in as cheerful a voice as he could muster when Maggie answered.

She laughed. "They aren't little monsters at all, Mr. Madison. Here, I'll let you talk to them."

Blake listened as she called for the kids.

"Hi, Dad." Drew came onto the line first. "Where you at?"

"Colt and I are taking some time off," he said, evading the question. "How's it going with you? You having fun?"

"Yeah. We went fishing today down at Baker's pond."

"Nice. Catch anything?"

"Two small sunnies. I didn't eat them, though." There was a short pause. "Dad, Whitney keeps talking about strange men being in the house taking Cait."

"You know how Whitney is." Blake closed his eyes as he tried to change the subject. "Is she close by? I want to talk to her."

"Yeah. Right here."

"Be good for Miss Maggie. I'll be home soon."

"When?"

"Soon. Put Whitney on."

"Where's Cait?"

"We'll talk when I get home. Love you, son."

He heard a loud sigh. "Here's Whit."

"Daddy?"

"Hey, pumpkin. Having fun?"

"We fished."

"I heard. Did you put the worms on the hook?"

She gurgled with laughter. "No. Yuck!"

"Well, you be good for Miss Maggie. Okay?"

"I miss you, Daddy."

Blake blinked his eyes to hold back the moisture. "Miss you, too, pumpkin. I'll be home soon."

"With Cait?"

He swallowed hard. "Yes. With Cait. Be good. Love you."

"I love you, too, Daddy."

When the phone disconnected, Blake lay straight back onto the bed for a moment and stared at the brown stains on the ceiling tiles.

Dear God, I promise to never take my life for granted again. Just bring her back safely. Please.

Was it really just yesterday that he and his wife had watched the sun set together with the kids playing in the leaves right beside them? Thoughts of Cait were like a hunger that gnawed at his heart and tore at his insides. He could never get enough of her, or fill the empty place her disappearance had left in his soul.

For better or worse, he had now joined that exclusive and terrifying fraternity of people who could look back and know the exact instant their life had changed forever. Tomorrow might bring events that would be remembered in future years as the best of his life—or they could reveal heartache and pain that would never dispel. But no matter what happened, good or bad, things would never be the same as they had been just twenty-four hours ago.

Blake sat back up and headed into the bathroom for a shower. After letting the water run, he was surprised to find it was actually hot and had halfway decent pressure. It gave him time to think, but he didn't necessarily like where his thoughts took him.

Where is Cait right now? How is she doing?

He closed his eyes and let the water stream over him as

her face came into vivid focus. She had a smile that put everyone at ease and expressive eyes that were always laughing. Joyful. Vibrant. It seemed almost impossible to think or believe that her life was in peril.

And just like that, her voice floated to him above the droning of the water, so clearly he almost looked over his shoulder to see if she were really there. He stood perfectly still, wanting to recall, yet cringing at the words that came to him. *Don't miss me too much.*

Hard to believe she had said those words just this morning—what seemed now both a lifetime and a moment ago. Did he tell her he loved her? Did she know he did? If only he could go back and start this day over. Bring back those precious moments of utter comfort and contentment. Never let her go. *Never.*

He sighed deeply—almost a groan—as he reminded himself that no amount of wishing was going to bring those moments back and nothing would ever be as it had. He pushed the feeling of hopelessness down before it could get footing, taking deep breaths to calm his heart. Slow, deep breaths to clear his mind.

With his mind still in overdrive, he thought back to the first time they had met. She had been a dripping wet reporter covering a crime scene he was investigating. He'd never really admitted it—even to himself—but she had captivated him from that very moment.

His mind bounded forward to the day he'd proposed, causing the memories to replay through his mind like a movie.

Cait had just finished testifying at a congressional hearing and was waiting for him by the Washington Monument. He'd snuck up behind her and grabbed her around the waist with one hand and the shoulders with the other. Drawing her up against him, he'd whispered in her ear. "Come here often?"

She'd tried to turn around and look up at him, but he held her firmly with her back pressed against him. "If that's your best pick-up line, you're going to be a lonely man," she'd said.

"Really? It works in the movies."

"Sorry. But, *no*."

"Okay. How about this?" He'd leaned down and whispered in her ear. "Hey, baby. Wanna ride in my truck?"

"Now you sound downright creepy," she'd said. "That's a definite *no*."

"Okay. Let me see… Close your eyes this time."

"All right. They're closed."

"Hey, sweetheart." He had let go of her then and backed away. "Are you free?"

"I don't know." She'd laughed, but continued to stand with her back to him. "That's a pretty broad question. When?"

"The rest of your life."

Whether it had been his words or the seriousness of his tone he didn't know, but she'd turned around with a perplexed expression on her face—and found him down on one knee with his kids, Drew on one side and Whitney on the other. All three held on to a sign that said, *Will you marry us?*

Blake's heart broke all over again at the memory. Her surprise and the children's pure delight at being a part of the occasion had forged a memory he would never forget as long as he lived.

Shaking his head to bring himself back to the present, Blake turned around and let the water pulsate on his neck. He forced himself to reflect on something else, anything to keep his thoughts from turning dark. Cait was not the kind of woman who would just give up and go along. She was strong. She would get through this.

But it never should have happened. It's my fault. Entirely.

His mind returned to their last conversation; what she had told him and what she hadn't told him—and it floored him to know there was almost as much of one as the other.

Had she known she was pregnant? Or just suspected it? Was she trying to figure out what his reaction would be? Did she not know he would be elated? The thought of it brought comfort and additional pain in unison. He put his hand on the shower wall to steady himself and almost groaned out loud.

Stop the self-pity bullshit. He abruptly turned off the water and stepped out of the shower. He didn't want to dwell on it, but he knew his inaction—or at least his lack of instinct that there was danger close—would remain one of his biggest regrets. Forever.

He dried himself quickly, knowing Colt would be back soon with the food. Having his best friend by his side was a blessing. There was an intensity and calmness about Colt that helped anyone near him feel a little safer and at ease, no matter the situation. That was one of the reasons Colt was still so sought after in the intelligence and security communities. He possessed a sort of innate, exuberant self-confidence and an extraordinary energy and drive that made him hard to keep up with—but easy to admire. The man would literally work until he dropped for anyone he called a friend.

The fact that Colt was quiet and reserved—some might even say brooding—made Blake's bond with him even stronger. Neither of them had ever been the type of men to crave conversation over silence, but after Colt had lost the woman he loved, he'd built up even more walls, grown even more detached, turned inward. That didn't bother Blake. Their friendship was solid. Their companionship rare. Words were not necessary to convey that each of them knew he had obtained a feverishly loyal and devoted friend in the other.

Blake heard the key in the door, just as his stomach growled, making him realize how hungry he actually was—and once again, how much he appreciated having Colt by his side.

Chapter 14

C olt left the room, walking swiftly. He had about a dozen calls to make and wanted to get back as soon as he could.

He hit the button for Podge first, just to see if there were any updates from the home base.

The report was pretty bleak. Podge gave some details on the previous findings, but overall, nothing new. No new sightings. No new leads.

Next, Colt dialed an old friend from one of the alphabet agencies to see if he had any new intel on Carlos or any idea where he could be holed up. His buddy said he'd snoop around and see if he could find anything, but had nothing to offer other than his condolences. Not exactly what Colt had been hoping for.

He opened the door of the restaurant and almost groaned out loud. A jam of people at least ten deep at all the registers. Patience was not a virtue he possessed, but he walked in and took his place in line. He didn't have much choice if he wanted to eat.

The line didn't move. Colt's mind began to wander and returned to a place it often did. The first day he'd met her.

"Sir, this is Jennifer Griffin. She's been assigned to accompany you on tonight's mission."

Colt thought Benton was playing a joke on him. A woman? On a special ops mission? Had to be a joke. And he wasn't in the mood to play along.

His gaze fell on a trim, athletic figure in fatigues and combat boots. As he tried to decide if this was a bad prank or for real, she stepped forward and held out her hand. "You can call me Griff, sir."

Her expression was steady and calm, and as unyielding as the grip of her handshake. When he looked into her liquid brown eyes, he suddenly felt short of breath. "Oka-a-y, Griff. You a journalist or something?"

The woman looked from him to the man who had introduced her as if surprised Colt didn't know her background.

"Sir, Lieutenant Griffin is an enabler with the Cultural Support Team we were briefed about yesterday."

Colt's eyes went from Benton to the woman and back again. He remembered zoning out when they'd started talking about CSTs accompanying them on missions. He hadn't really thought they were serious.

"I'm here to make it easier for you guys to do your job on a mission by engaging the female population."

It was uncanny the way she made direct eye contact when talking, as if drilling down into his very soul. It made him want to keep her talking, just so he could stare into those eyes a little longer.

"She's also an expert on Islamic culture and speaks Urdu, Peshwa, and Arabic," Benton said.

"So you can translate for us?" Colt finally remembered to let go of her hand.

"I understand you have a translator." Her lips rose into a confused smile as her gaze darted over to Benton with a look that said, this-isn't-what-I-expected. "But yes, if the occasion arises, I can translate for you."

"Sir. Sir? Can I help you?" The frustrated voice of the woman behind the counter brought Colt back to the present.

"Oh, yeah. Sorry. Give me two number fives." When his gaze met the cashier's, he noticed she had deep brown eyes.

"For here or to go?"

He blinked, still staring into her eyes. They were big. Dark as coffee and framed with long lashes.

"Sir. For. Here. Or. To. Go?"

"Sorry again. To go."

She rolled her cat-like eyes with a look of pure annoyance, took his money, and turned to get his food.

Damn. Wake up, Nick. Get your head on straight.

The images that had come back to him were so vivid, they had seemed real. Maybe because Cait was so close to him. Or maybe because this was a hostage situation. In any event, he had to get beyond it and move on. Now was not the time to be thinking about the past.

A few minutes later, he carried the bag of food across the parking lot and through the hotel room door. Blake was sitting on the bed with a towel wrapped around his waist. He looked up and forced a smile, but an unspoken pain was alive and glowing in his eyes.

"You forgot to shave," Colt teased as he dropped the bags on one of the beds and began rummaging through them.

"I didn't bring a razor. I'm not on a fucking business trip."

Colt raised his eyes from the food and lowered them again before speaking. It was so unusual to hear Blake swear. "Your disposition hasn't improved, but you sure do smell better. Here."

Blake took the sandwich from his extended hand. "Sorry, bro."

"Accepted."

Colt knew Blake felt helpless, and that that was the reason for his surliness. Already, he looked older. Worn. Tired. Eyes hollowed by strain and his loss. His wife was in someone else's hands, and he didn't want to be sitting around in a hotel doing nothing. But he was going to have to accept it. Colt had a feeling this wasn't going to be resolved in mere hours, and maybe not even days.

"You get to talk to the kids?"

"Yeah," Blake responded casually, but his hand shook slightly as he lifted his bottle of water.

Colt watched the tremor in silent agony. It was hard to see a man he had such deep respect and love for in so much pain. "They doing okay?"

"As good as they can be. They're having fun spending the weekend away from home, but..."

"We'll know more tomorrow," Colt said, ripping into his sandwich. "I have a good feeling about tomorrow."

Blake didn't respond to that. "What did Podge say?"

Colt mulled over what he should say as he chewed. Blake knew he'd been getting situational reports or SITREPs from everyone on the team. There was no use denying it. "Nothing of significance in the car. Hair fibers proved Cait was there, but that's about it."

"No signs of a struggle?" Blake's voice cracked.

"No." Colt didn't elaborate. He knew he didn't need to. Blake knew as well as anyone that the lack of a struggle could mean she was drugged, unconscious, or being threatened with a gun or knife. It could even mean she was already dead, but neither of them believed that.

"Anything more at the hotel? Video?"

"No. They stayed at a crappy hotel like this one. So nothing on that side except for the descriptions from the workers."

"Which is?"

"Two Hispanic males and at least one female." Colt took another bite of his sandwich. "Only one man checked in, but a cleaning lady said she saw two. Another housekeeper thought there were two women in another room but no one knows for sure."

Blake nodded while staring at the wall. It seemed to bring some comfort to him that Cait was at least under the care of another woman.

Colt balled up the paper from his sandwich and tossed it into the trashcan across the room. "Get some sleep, brother."

"Yeah. Right."

"I need you sharp." Colt pulled his shirt over his head. "If they keep driving, we're going to have to keep driving, so stretch out and rest while you can."

"Why hasn't he called yet? Maybe we're going down the wrong path."

"It hasn't even been twelve hours. This isn't Hollywood, dude. It doesn't work like that."

Just then, Blake's phone rang. He lunged for where it rested on the stand beside the bed and brought it to his ear without looking to see who was calling. "Madison here."

Colt could just barely make out the conversation. "Mr.

Madison, this is Chris Rays with CNN. How are you doing tonight?"

Blake's eyes darted up to Colt's as he raked his free hand through his hair. "Where did you get this number?"

"I just received a tip that your wife has been kidnapped and I'm calling to confirm."

"That doesn't answer my question."

"Well…I got it with the tip. I'm calling to see if you can confirm or deny that your wife is missing."

Colt shook his head and warned Blake with his eyes not to say anything.

"Hold on a second, let me check." Not wanting to get caught in a lie, Blake hurriedly pulled his wallet from his back pocket and flipped it to a picture of Caitlin. "Sorry to disappoint you, but I'm looking at my wife as we speak."

A long silence ensued. "May I talk to her?"

"I have no idea who you are so, no, you cannot talk to my wife. Good night."

Blake disconnected and then fell backward onto the bed mumbling a string of expletives.

"I'd better give Podge a call." Colt pulled out his phone just as it began to ring. "Hey, buddy."

"We got our first call here," Podge said.

"Yeah, Blake did, too. He stalled them so they don't have anything concrete, but it was CNN so they'll probably go with a story anyway."

"I haven't seen anything hit the air yet, but it's only a matter of time."

Colt could hear Podge talking to someone else and then

he came back on the line. "I have a couple of guys posted out at the gate in case we get some nosy newshounds here at the house."

"Good deal. We're hitting the sack for a few hours."

"Okay. Catch some Zs. Talk later."

When Colt ended the call and looked up from his phone, Blake was sitting on the edge of the bed again with his elbows on his knees. "You okay?"

"I'm fine." His voice was not so much calm as toneless, as if he were already thinking of other things.

"It's kind of good news, right?" Colt stood up and undid his belt. "Knowing we're on the right track."

"Yeah." Blake rubbed his forehead. "Good news. I can only imagine what the morning news programs are gonna do with this."

"Well, they don't have anything yet. Who knows what Carlos is going to feed them, but they're not going to have any actual facts."

Blake faked a laugh. "Like that's ever stopped them."

Colt knew there was nothing he could say to make the inevitable any easier. "I'm going to hit the shower. Get some sleep."

"What time we pulling out?"

"I figured zero three hundred hours. That'll give us a few hours of sleep."

"Not that I'll need it," Blake said, pushing buttons on his phone. "But I'll set my alarm."

"Night, buddy.

Colt turned off the lights and headed to the bathroom. When he finished with his shower, Blake was dressed except for his shoes. He was lying on his back, staring at the ceiling, looking like he was wide awake.

Throwing on a tee shirt, Colt climbed into bed and remembered nothing else until Blake was shaking him awake. "It's time, man."

Colt opened one eye and looked at the clock. "I got five more minutes, bro."

"You said we'd get back on the road at zero three hundred."

"That's not what I meant." Colt stretched. "I meant we'd *get up* at zero three hundred."

Blake didn't respond other than to finish throwing his things into a bag. When he got to the door, he talked over his shoulder. "I'll grab us something to eat and wait for you in the truck."

"And coffee," Colt yelled after him. "Big. Black. Coffee."

Hearing no response but the slamming of the door, Colt got up, threw on his clothes, and brushed his teeth. He rubbed his hand over his whiskers. Despite how he looked, he felt refreshed and ready to go. But he couldn't help wondering about Blake. Had he slept at all?

By the time he made it to the truck, Blake was just getting in with a bag of food and two large coffees.

"Thank heavens for all-night fast food joints." Colt took the coffee and then unwrapped his sandwich. "Breakfast of champions right here. Thanks."

"Let's go," was all Blake said.

Colt pulled back onto the highway and devoured his meal

without talking. When the last crumb was gone, he crumpled up the trash and reached for the paper bag to dispose of it.

"I'll get that. Just drive."

"I can multi-task, believe it or not. Been doing this for years."

"Just drive," Blake repeated.

Colt was about to respond when the phone began to ring in the console. It was a number he didn't recognize.

"Put it on speaker," Blake said before Colt had even picked it up.

Colt's gaze went to the clock on the console, wondering who would be calling at this hour. He picked up the phone and put it to his ear, refusing to make eye contact with Blake. It might not be good news. "Colt here."

"Colt. This is Brody. Podge is getting some shut-eye. He wanted me to give you a call and make sure you're back on the road.

"Yes, sir. We're back in the saddle. What phone are you on?"

"Oh, sorry. Got a new phone and number."

"Okay. I've got it now. Anything new on your end?"

"Negative. Following up on some leads, but nothing new yet."

"What's he saying?" Blake hit Colt in the shoulder.

"Okay. Keep us posted."

"Wait. I need to—" Blake almost grabbed the phone from his hand.

Colt disconnected and looked over at Blake. "Sorry, man. He hung up."

Blake shrugged. "If it was Podge, I wanted to tell him to help himself to the apple pie. It might as well not go to waste."

"You kidding me?" Colt laughed. "You think Podge and those guys needed an invitation to eat homemade pie? It's probably long gone." Colt wanted to ask why in the hell Blake hadn't brought the pie along but stopped himself. His friend had had other things on this mind. But damn, he could sure eat some of Cait's homemade pie right about now.

"Yeah. I guess you're right."

"Here, make yourself useful. That was Brody with a new number. Add it to my contacts."

"Yessir, boss." Blake took the phone and copied the number into his own phone before adding it to Colt's.

"So, why's he calling in the middle of the night?" Blake studied Colt as if to see if he could uncover any hint of what had been said. "Did he have anything new? Did Carlos make contact yet?"

"No. Basically, he just wanted to make sure we hadn't overslept."

Blake shook his head. "Yeah, right. Sleep."

"Did you get any, man?" Colt studied Blake's sullen face. "We're in for the long haul now."

"I'm good."

Blake let out his breath, apparently exasperated that the phone call had brought no new intelligence. Their theory of how this was going to go down relied on Carlos making contact. If he didn't, it could mean... Colt pushed those thoughts from his mind.

"You probably didn't sleep much. Why don't you take a combat nap while I'm driving? You need to recharge."

"I said, I'm good, *Mother*."

Colt shook his head. "I hope you don't make me regret bringing you along."

"Excuse me?"

"You heard me."

Blake turned his head toward the window. "I'm good. You don't have to worry about me."

"Come on, man." Colt leaned forward and turned down the radio. "Now I know you're shitting me. You *can't* be good. No one would be."

"I should have seen it coming." Blake's voice trembled slightly as he stared out the window. "I should have known."

"About the kidnapping?"

"No. That she... That *we* were having a baby."

Colt's breath caught in his throat. Blake wasn't the type to share personal things. He just wasn't that kind of guy. And of all the topics in the world, this was one Colt didn't think Blake would want to discuss with him. Then again, maybe it was something he wanted to get off his chest.

"What do you mean?"

"She's been... I don't know, sentimental, reflective. Emotional. I guess it was the hormones." He put a hand to his temple and rubbed. "I wish to God she didn't have to go through this alone."

"She's strong." Colt tried to console Blake. "You know she is. And you know what else?"

Blake shook his head.

"I bet you any amount of money, the only thing she's worried about right this very minute is that *you're* worrying about *her*."

Blake cracked half a smile. "You're probably right about that." The smile disappeared almost instantly and turned into a frown of concern.

"So stop it. Worrying about her isn't going to do any good. It will only sap your strength."

"Promise me something." Blake turned his blue eyes toward Colt as if he hadn't heard a word he'd just said.

"Anything, brother. You know that."

"You remember my sister, Becky, right?"

Colt laughed. "You kidding me? Broke my heart when she got married."

"If anything happens to me, make sure everything goes smoothly with getting the kids to her."

Colt's gaze jerked over to him. "What are you talking about?"

"Beck and I have talked about it—especially after the Kessler thing. It's all in writing. Just make sure it's a smooth transition. You know, keep the government red tape crap and stress to a minimum."

"I don't think you have to worry—"

"Yeah. I know, but just in case." He stared out the window as if he were still thinking. "And as far as the house goes, contact Walter Snow and find a way to merge it straight into the business so you can keep it. It can just become the main headquarters. It practically is already."

"I don't know why you're talking like this, dude. I hope

you're not thinking about doing anything crazy."

"You know how fast things like this go to shit." Blake paused. "And it *is* Carlos. I'm just thinking ahead."

"Well, *I'm* thinking a few years from now we'll be looking back on this as a little blip in our history. Nothing more."

Blake exhaled. "Yeah. I hope so."

Colt was all for making contingency plans, but he didn't like looking at worst-case scenarios. He felt like it was planning for bad luck. "If it makes you feel better, I'll take care of everything, but nothing is going to happen."

Blake nodded and looked out the window.

Since the conversation had waned, Colt reached down and tried to find a radio station. When he finally found one that wasn't just static, he turned it up.

"Your favorite kind of music, right?"

Blake didn't answer but he did finally put his head back and close his eyes. Colt knew he wasn't sleeping—not the way his foot kept tapping against the floor mat. The lack of conversation in the truck made Colt's thoughts wander about what might be happening to Caitlin at the moment.

If her captors were far enough ahead to get past the police near Staunton, then they were most likely headed this way. He looked at each car that he passed. She could literally be mere miles—or *feet* from them at this very moment. How were her captors treating her? They had probably been hired to deliver her safely to a pre-determined meeting place—and would know better than to upset Carlos by hurting her. It gave Colt some measure of relief to think that she might be safe, at least for now. But he knew time was running out.

Headlights and taillights seemed to merge and blur as mile after mile passed with little to no conversation. Blake remained restless but lost in his own thoughts, so Colt let his mind wander as well. It ended up where it often did.

"Quiet guys, here comes the NFG."

"Ha. Ha. Very funny." Griff *strode in and plopped down on the picnic table where a group of men had gathered. "That's not sexist or anything. Where's the HR Department in this place anyway? I want to file a complaint."*

"What's sexist about it? It stands for New Fucking GAL."

"Good one." Griff *twisted the cap off a bottle of water and took a long drink before giving* Colt *one of her deep, soul-searching looks. "Especially coming from the OFG."*

"OFG? What's an OFG?"

"Old. Fucking. Goat."

A roar of laughter filled the air, and Colt *knew he would never hear the end of that one. He couldn't believe a female could mix so effortlessly with this particular group of men—not only on missions but also during downtime when they could be brutal with one another, even by male standards. She could dish it out and she could take it. Bantering, ribbing, joking—just like she was one of the guys.*

"We there yet?" Blake stirred in the seat beside him, jolting Colt back to the present.

His gaze shot to the dashboard. The needle was closing in on a quarter of a tank of gas. His eyes flicked to the rearview mirror where the sky was beginning to lighten to the east.

"We need to make a fueling stop."

"You mean you have to piss from drinking all of that coffee, right?"

Colt looked over at his friend, whose eyes were still closed. "Don't you?"

"Yeah. Let's make it quick."

"Guess that means the stack of pancakes at the Waffle House I've been dreaming about for the last hundred miles is out of the question."

Blake's eyes were open now and had a don't-you-dare-even-think-about-it look in them as Colt shifted over to a ramp and headed toward the glow of a truck stop sign.

"I'll pump," Blake said. "You go do your business."

"Thanks, bro. You hungry?"

"Grab me a coffee. I'll be in to use the facilities in a sec."

Colt nodded and headed inside. After using the restroom, he bought an armload of munchies, two four-packs of Red Bull, a couple of pre-packaged sandwiches, and two large cups of coffee. He had just finished paying and was trying to figure out how to carry it all when Blake stepped up behind him.

"Let's go." Blake grabbed the coffees and headed toward the truck but talked over his shoulder. "By the way, CNN called again."

Blake said the words so calmly and businesslike that it took Colt a minute to grasp what he'd disclosed.

"What? What'd you tell them?"

"I told him I had another call coming in and had to go." Blake's phone went off again as they talked. He sat the coffees on the hood and glanced at the number, then hit *Ignore*. "They found someone at the local police station who confirmed they're investigating a case, so they're hot and heavy on it now."

"Shit. This doesn't change things, but it sure does compli-
cate them." Colt opened Blake's door before walking around
to the other side of the truck. *The last thing we need is to have those
knuckleheads showing up, distracting the team, slowing us down.*

Despite the bad news, Colt took the time to pause and
take in the scenery before climbing into the cab. He found
that stepping back a moment and looking at the world around
him helped to center him—and this was his favorite time of
day. A sliver of moon still hung in the sky, while a slice of va-
nilla and cotton candy pink had cut through the darkness on
the eastern horizon. The dawning of a new day. What would
it bring? Good things? Or bad?

He slid into the seat and handed Blake a sandwich while
ripping the paper off of his. "Eat up. Good stuff."

Blake stared at it a moment and then took a hesitant taste
as Colt devoured his in a couple of bites. When Blake's phone
vibrated again, he sighed with exasperation. "Call Podge. See
if he has anything new. I'd like to know if anything has hit the
morning shows yet." By the time he pulled his phone out, it
had stopped vibrating. "Probably the same guy."

"Nah. Podge would have called if they'd found something."

At that moment, Colt's phone began to ring.

"Put it on speaker." Blake's blue eyes glared at Colt.

"I don't know how." Colt picked up the phone. "What's
up, Podge?"

"We had a possible sighting."

"Where?"

"Tennessee. Outside Nashville."

"So the FBI is on board?"

"Yep. As soon as we heard they'd crossed the state line—we're filling them in now."

"What's going on?"

Colt lowered the phone and talked to Blake. "Possible sighting outside of Nashville."

He put the phone back to his ear. "What happened?"

"An off-duty police officer was eating at a fast-food restaurant when he noticed two women go into the restroom together."

"Note to police officer—that's not unusual," Colt said blandly.

"No. But after they walked out, he saw one return."

"Oka-a-a-y." Colt still didn't see what had raised the officer's curiosity. "Did he see the vehicle?"

"No. It was on the other side of the building. But the woman who came back in was Hispanic, and he just had a gut feeling about the other one."

"Gut feeling? Like what?"

"What's he saying?" Blake grabbed Colt's arm and shook him.

"He couldn't explain it," Podge said. "He didn't act on it until he went to work and started nosing around BOLOs. That's when he ran across this case and called. We don't have any info back yet on security images, but they're looking at them now."

"Okay, buddy. Thanks."

"I'm not done."

"Okay... What else?"

"The press. We've gotten more calls, and they're hanging out down by the gate."

"*Fuck*." Colt hit the steering wheel. "Blake's been getting calls, too. Tell them we'll have a statement in an hour."

"What's it going to say?"

"If I knew that, I'd tell you right now. I'll call you later."

"Wait. I have an idea."

"Go ahead."

"What if I play the same game Carlos is playing?"

"What do you mean?"

"Leak some information. Give them a nibble to send them on a wild goose chase. It will take them time to track it down and sort it out. If we don't talk, they'll say we're hiding something and do a story anyway."

"Sounds like a plan. I knew we hired you for a good reason."

"Thanks, boss. I've got Danner and Michaels manning phones and making calls to customers to get ahead of this thing for the company. We're going to take a hit, but at least they'll hear it from us, not the media."

"Remind me to give you a raise when this is over."

"Just bring her back," Podge said in a low voice. "That's raise enough for me."

"Copy that."

Blake didn't ask any questions once Colt hung up, but unspoken, angry accusations were being hurled from the icy depths of his blue eyes as he waited for a briefing.

Colt explained what had been reported in Nashville, all the while examining every vehicle he passed. He noticed Blake was doing the same thing.

"What's the plan for handling the press?" Blake had put two and two together on that part of the conversation.

"Podge is going to feed them some juicy tidbits to get them off track. It will hopefully give us a couple of hours of peace and quiet."

Blake nodded. "Sounds like a plan. If I get any more calls, I'll just tell them to call Podge for updates."

"Yeah. He'll update them, all right." As Colt's gaze shifted to the rearview mirror, he saw that the rising sun had set the sky ablaze with a brilliant shade of red.

"That's quite a scene behind us."

Blake turned around in the seat and studied the sunrise a moment, then turned back and stared straight ahead without comment.

Colt knew exactly what he was thinking. *Why is the sun coming up as if nothing is wrong?*

"I have a good feeling about today." Colt tried to make his voice match the words—not what he was actually thinking. "It's going to be a good day."

Blake didn't answer because his phone was vibrating. Assuming it was just a call from a reporter, he fished it out of his pocket and pushed the button to put it on speaker, shooting a this-is-how-it's-done look at Colt.

"Madison here."

"Meester Madison," a jovial voice responded with a heavy Spanish accent. "They tell me you've lost something."

Chapter 15

Colt jerked the truck over to the side of the road and started punching numbers on his phone as Blake continued the conversation. "What do you want, Carlos?" Blake's voice sounded calm, even though it was clear by the look on his face that he was not.

Blake's question was followed by loud laughter, but the merriment stopped abruptly. "I want you to suffer, *señor*. As I have suffered."

Blake did not pause. "Then let's make a trade. Me, for her." His voice was so calm, Blake may as well have been discussing the weather. But his face revealed a look of bone-deep distress.

"Ha. You are joking with me." Ice cubes tinkled in the background as if Carlos were making himself an early morning drink.

"Where is she, Carlos?" Blake's voice was no longer composed.

"You know it does not make me happy when my plans change, but I think having your young wife instead of your kids might be a good thing."

"The offer still stands." Blake's voice sounded weary and strained. "Me for her."

"No. I am anxious to meet your lovely wife."

It sounded like he took a sip of his drink. "I have heard much about her."

Colt was trying to listen to the conversation while connecting to the lead investigator at the FBI. He motioned for Blake to keep Carlos talking, yet he was afraid what the drug lord's words were doing to his friend. At least now they had confirmation that Caitlin was not yet in Carlos's possession.

"What do you want exactly, Carlos? Tell me where she is."

"That I cannot tell you. But I will be meeting her in person." He took another leisurely swallow. "Soon."

Blake looked at Colt with an expression so full of alarm it pinched Colt's heart. Given a fair shake, man-to-man, Colt would put Blake up against anyone. But his friend was powerless right now. Carlos had known exactly how to hurt him and had planned it well. He could not be causing more pain than if he'd cut Blake open and pulled out his beating heart.

Actually, he had a feeling Blake would prefer that means of torture to this one.

"I can promise you, Carlos, you will be sorry about this. This isn't a game."

Those words were greeted by loud, boisterous laughter. "No. The pain in your voice, it is like music to my ears. I will never be sorry to hear that."

"Any pain you hear is from the fact that you can't handle this like a man, Carlos. Is this how you got to be so powerful? By picking on innocent women instead of dealing with things like a man?"

Colt was able to whisper a few words to the agent on the line as the sound of a glass crashing hard against a table resonated over Blake's phone, followed by a string of expletives in Spanish. "I am going to see that you suffer as I have suffered. Do you know what it feels like to lose a child?"

"I had nothing to do with your son's death, Carlos. I wasn't even in the same state at the time."

"But you were the cause of it! And you will pay for it."

"If you want me to pay for it, then trade me for her. Be a man."

"You think you are more of a man than me?" Carlos's voice cracked with rage. "When I am done, you will be begging me for mercy! Then we will see who is the man."

Even though he was still in the middle of his own whispered phone conversation, Colt heard the wrath in Carlos's response. He knew Blake had to walk a fine line. Carlos was renowned for his inability to control his anger—many a man had died because of his hair-trigger temper.

"Okay, Carlos. What's next?" Blake's face was contorted with suppressed agony, but he somehow managed to control his voice. It was back to its usual composed, poised tone. "Why are you calling me?"

Carlos seemed to regain control, as well. "This is just a courtesy call, *amigo*. So that you do not have to worry that your wife is in good hands…" He laughed, but even through the phone it was easy to tell there was no humor in it—only malicious pleasure. "She will be in *very* good hands."

Cradling his own phone between shoulder and ear and holding the steering wheel with his left hand, Colt reached out to grab Blake's arm, afraid of what he might do or say.

Blake shook him off and leaned forward as he shouted

into the phone. "If you touch one hair on her head, Carlos, I can promise, you will die!"

The phone went silent.

Blake went from having his head almost even with the dashboard to slamming it back against the headrest, breathing like he had just run a race. His eyes were closed as he moved his head back and forth, seemingly trying to keep from seeing images that would not stop playing in his mind.

"We'll find her, brother."

Blake nodded with his eyes still closed, but Colt could tell from the set of his jaw and his pursed lips that they were both thinking the same thing.

Would it be in time?

Chapter 16

Cait knew they had to be getting close to Mexico—and Carlos—and understood she had little chance of surviving once that happened. She had to find a way to escape. They had been driving day and night, only stopping for food, gas, and to use the restroom. Most of the time she had a towel over her head, making it hard for her to tell from the sun what time of day it was or how much time had passed.

Today was no different, but she had listened to the steady cadence of the windshield wipers for hours. Now there was the additional sound of thunder and wind, and the anxious mutterings of the two men in the front seat as they talked about the severity of the weather.

Maria whimpered after a particularly loud burst of thunder, and even from beneath the towel, Caitlin saw the brilliant flash of lightning that followed. The storm had such a frightening violence to it, Cait feared it was an omen.

She had heard Maria ask for a restroom break more than an hour earlier, and they still had not stopped. Were they nearing the border? She began to squirm in her seat as if uncomfortable.

"What is wrong, *señora?*"

"I have to go to the bathroom."

Maria spoke in Spanish to the men, but Cait could not make out their murmured response.

"*Sí*. Rest stop in two miles," she finally heard Juan say in Spanish. That was followed by another whispered conversation in the front seat as if they were deciding how to handle letting her use the public restroom.

Cait's mind raced. This could be her chance. She felt the van slowing as they exited the highway and blinked against the light as Maria pulled the towel from her eyes. She leaned close with a warning. "They will kill you if you try anything." Maria's eyes were full of concern. "They can deliver you dead or alive." Cait nodded as Maria cut the ties from her wrists. "You must stay with me."

Cait nodded again as the two men turned around and accentuated Maria's words by showing her the blades of their knives. Juan went so far as to make a slicing motion at his neck to show her he meant business. She had no doubt they would kill her—even in a public place—if it meant protecting their boss. She had heard stories that involved crimes much worse than that—and local agencies, fearing for their lives, always turned a blind eye. No one ever faced charges for the crimes, even if there were numerous witnesses.

Maria exited the van first and waited for Cait to follow. A light rain was falling, but it felt wonderful, refreshing. Clean. Caitlin tried to appear meek and compliant as she walked beside Maria, but she lifted her head before entering, searching for the security cameras she knew must be in place. If anyone had a reason to look at them, she wanted to make sure they saw her face. She glanced back at the van and saw that the men were following closely behind. Were they going to the restroom, as well? Or were they simply going to wait for her?

Caitlin knew this was her final chance. It was now or never. They were too close to the border for her to wait another minute. She caught a glimpse of a large map in front of her and tried to find the *You Are Here* icon, but Maria took her by the arm and pulled her inside before she was able to locate it.

The restroom was large, with eight stalls on one side and a row of sinks on the other—and it was crowded with people apparently seeking refuge from the storm.

Caitlin went into the first open door, which had occupants on each side. "Do not try anything," Maria whispered as she proceeded to another stall farther down. It was unusual for Maria not to watch Cait the whole time, but the look on the woman's face indicated she needed to go, urgently.

Caitlin locked the stall door but otherwise did not move. The woman in the stall next to hers talked loudly on the phone and sounded irritated and in a hurry. Caitlin considered signaling to her under the stall but was afraid she would scream and alert Maria or the men outside.

Instead, as the woman flushed, Caitlin slipped out of her shoes and left them sitting in front of the toilet. As soon as she heard the woman's stall door open, Cait laid down on her back and pulled herself into that stall. The woman was in such a hurry, she never went to the sinks or stopped talking on the phone. Once in the empty stall, Cait hurried out and then froze. Should she try to run and sneak past the men? What if they were standing right outside, watching the door? She wouldn't put it past them. She knew they did not trust her.

Anyway, where would she go? She could run to the back lot…to where the big rigs were parked and try to get a ride from a truck driver. But wasn't that the first place they would look? And what if the truck drivers thought she was a prostitute looking for a ride? What if they were loyal to Carlos—or feared him enough to hand her over?

She heard Maria pulling up her pants and knew time was running out.

Run or stay? Stay or run? God help me!

She stood practically frozen with fear and anger at her own indecision when an *OUT OF ORDER* sign on the door at the very end of the row of stalls caught her eye. Moving quietly, she went into that stall and closed the door.

When Maria flushed, she used the sound as cover to latch the door, and then drew her feet up while sitting on the toilet. She heard laughter as more people came into the bathroom, and then the sound of Maria exiting her stall and washing her hands.

Caitlin closed her eyes. The thump of her heart pounding in her ears became so overwhelming, she expected Maria to hear it and find her at any moment. She watched through a crack in the door as Maria finished washing her hands and turned back toward the stalls. She was now out of Cait's view, but she could hear the woman bend down. She must have seen the shoes under the stall door because all she said was, "You are taking a long time."

Caitlin's heart raced, wondering how long Maria would wait before checking again. She soon got her answer. Maria knocked on the stall door. "Are you all right, *señora*? Are you sick again?" When she received no response, Maria must have finally bent down lower to investigate.

Again, Caitlin waited, holding her breath. When the discovery came, Maria screamed so loudly that other women rushed to her aid. The Hispanic woman did not wait around to explain the cause of her alarm. She rushed out the door, sobbing and whimpering in anguished panic.

Now the hunt would begin. Caitlin took deep breaths, knowing this would be the last place they would look. They would expect her to run, to try to hitch a ride and get away. Right now, they were probably searching high and low for her, for anyone who might have seen her. Surely, they would be drawing attention to themselves. Would anyone think to call the police? Or would they go about their business, absorbed in their own little worlds?

Suddenly, her worst nightmare came true. Instead of searching outside as she had expected them to, she heard Pedro talking in loud tones outside the ladies' room. It was clear he did not believe Maria.

Caitlin heard women scream as he burst into the room. Seeing the locked stall door where Caitlin had been, he kicked it, apparently not believing she wasn't still hiding in there. It crashed open and bounced against the wall in a crescendo of noise that made Caitlin put her hands over her ears.

But a loud voice interrupted the rampage. "What are you doing? I'm calling the police."

Caitlin saw Pedro in the mirror as his gaze swept the room and landed on the door she was behind. His eyes blazed with rage, his face was contorted in fury. She held her breath as he stared, trying not to whimper at the savage look on his face.

"Get out or I'm calling the police." A woman right behind Pedro had her phone out and was pushing numbers.

Pedro growled and turned around to leave. Caitlin wanted to run to the woman and beg her to call the police, but the lady turned and followed Pedro out the door.

Caitlin kept her head tucked to her knees, trying to regain control of her heart rate. She felt like she was going to pass out from the pure terror that enveloped her. Just outside the door, women continued to come into the bathroom, some commenting on the broken door, but none aware of what had commenced just a few minutes earlier.

Caitlin remained perfectly quiet for what felt like hours. Would Pedro have given up yet? Had they left? Or were they still searching outside? She felt sweat trickling down her face, but she refused to move. She had to pee but was afraid to do that, too. Finally, when the room grew quiet for a few minutes, she relieved herself and then drew her feet back up when she heard someone enter.

Every time she got up the nerve to step out and ask someone for help, a voice would remind her that Carlos had a wide reach. Some loved him. Some hated him. But all feared him.

Would anyone help her?

Who could she trust?

Just go out and tell the first person you see to call the police. Someone will help you.

Then she would think. *What if Carlos has people here, just waiting for me to come out of my hiding place? What if innocent people die in the process of me running for safety?*

That thought alone was enough to keep her silent.

She wanted to hear Blake's reassuring voice—she almost expected to. How close was he?

Then reality set in. How would Blake know where she was? How would he even know who had taken her? She put her face in her hands and tried to stifle her sobs.

Blake, I'm sorry to be so weak. I don't know what to do.

Her weakness made her think of his strength...of his toughness, no matter the situation. He had survived much more hopeless circumstances than this. He had been pinned down in a foreign country, fighting for thirteen hours while waiting for the United States to send reinforcements, which never came. Despite circumstances that seemed insurmountable, he had fought on—and survived.

Chapter 17

Carlos straightened the collar of his tailored suit while walking up the steps toward the wide, sweeping arches of his palatial mission-style mansion.

He motioned for two of his bodyguards to follow him into the house, allowing the other three to keep watch outside. Even though the compound had a fence and an army of security people patrolling it, he did not feel safe without his contingent of personal protection. He had picked these men from hundreds of others because of their vigilance, their raw fighting skills—and most of all, their loyalty to him. These were battle-hardened men with nerves of steel that could react with fierce ingenuity under fire. They were his *pistoleros*—his gunmen—and he relied on them for his very survival.

The men who had earned this coveted position possessed another admirable quality, as well—they enjoyed violence. Carlos needed that. He had a reputation to defend—a reputation for directing his organization with an iron fist and controlling his employees with violent intimidation. He did not tolerate rebellion, either overt or covert—or even simply suspected. If a leak was alleged, or if a member or associate failed to act as expected, these were the men who undertook the removal quickly...and permanently.

Plus, it was no secret that he *needed* to be surrounded by

the very best. In addition to the authorities who were always harassing him, he faced a wide array of adversaries—from the younger dealers trying to work their way up the ladder, to the older ones who had scores to settle.

Of their own accord, these five men inspired fear in others—and showed their loyalty to Carlos—by wearing skull-fragment necklaces, the pieces of which had been provided by the last drug dealer who tried to take their boss's place.

Yes, many people wanted Carlos dead…too many to count. He could trust no one completely, but he believed these five men would die for him—if for no other reason than they knew the alternative would not be as quick and easy as being killed in a firefight.

As he reached the top step, Carlos turned and gazed out over the manicured lawn and lush gardens of his estate, then farther, to the place where the brown desert met the skyline. His holdings were vast, the boundary of his property being far beyond where his eyes could see. He owned or could purchase anything and everything his heart desired, yet it occurred to him that being wealthy created a sort of loneliness and isolation that a poorer man never had to worry about. He quickly dismissed the thought and even laughed out loud. He could have any woman he wanted at any time—more than one at a time if he so desired. No poor man could do that.

But Carlos had a lot of responsibility too. He was *the* top narcotics *padrinos* of Mexico, controlling everything along a two-hundred-mile stretch of the border in both Texas and New Mexico. That meant more than fifty tons of cocaine a year being smuggled for the Colombians—not to mention the incalculable amounts of marijuana and heroin that were the mainstay of his operation. He often raked in at least two hundred million a week, with a portion of it going back into the business as payoffs and bribes. Most of it, however, he used to treat himself lavishly and buy whatever he desired.

But having everything money could buy was not enough to satisfy his entrepreneurial drive. He had recently expanded into another lucrative enterprise—one that most people in the United States were not even aware of yet. It was a natural progression for his illegal operation that required no additional assets or time, yet yielded lots of new capital. He had simply directed his network of experienced smugglers to provide logistical support to Islamic extremists trying to enter the U.S. The venture paid so well that Carlos had already expanded his services, creating stash areas for newly arrived immigrants to lay low in a small crossroads town about fifty miles from El Paso.

Until recently, the new undertaking had sailed along without a hitch, but last week he'd been told someone from the U.S. government may have infiltrated the ring of smuggled terrorists. It could have been a false report or just a rumor, but Carlos had come too far to take any chances. His plot to kidnap Blake Madison's children was put into action earlier than he'd planned so he could divert the attention of the American media and counter-terrorism professionals from what was happening right under their noses.

As far as what the Islamic terrorists had planned, Carlos didn't ask and didn't want to know. His responsibility ended when they reached their destination. They didn't interfere in his business—and he wasn't going to interfere in theirs.

After waiting for the door to be opened for him, Carlos stepped inside to the large, open foyer. Sun trickled in through the floor-to-ceiling windows, causing the three white pillars to reflect off the shiny marble floors. The house immediately became a beehive of activity as his staff rushed to see if there was anything he needed.

Carlos was a talented businessman, but his success in reaching the pinnacle of organized crime and power was not simply the product of his entrepreneurial skills or leadership ability. His violent temper and willingness for bloodshed is what had placed him in a class all by himself. Everyone knew that—except perhaps Carlos himself.

It is better for six innocent men to die than one guilty person to live. That was his philosophy. If a family of four had to die because one person would not talk, so be it. He ordered killings at the slightest suspicions that people were informants, and sometimes watched to make sure they took place. Some called it a sociopathic trait—he called it part of a day's work.

He felt no guilt about what it had taken to get to the top or the lives that had been sacrificed to make it happen. In his mind, he deserved everything he possessed. He had, after all, endured growing up in a border town in the midst of harsh political and economic circumstances. His ancestors had made a living with their petty smuggling, but he was destined for so much more. Never again would a Valdez be working as a servant for the *gringos* in America.

No, if those who came before him could only see the

volume of cocaine and marijuana he transported across the border, the number of aircraft he owned, and the size of the airplanes and their cargo…they would not believe it. Of course, to achieve that, he had more than four hundred murders attributed to his cartel, but that was just a part of doing business.

"I have work to do," he said in Spanish as he headed toward his office in the back of the house. His bodyguards scattered the other workers with a wave of their hands, except for kitchen waitstaff. They remained close by in case he decided he wanted something to eat or drink.

Everything is going exactly as planned so far. Carlos laughed to himself. *Stupid Americans.*

They made it easy. So sure of themselves. So ignorant of the evil that existed in the world around them. So confident that their innocence would be a shield to the darkness and violence that lurked around every corner.

Carlos's cell phone rang just as he entered the large hallway that stretched the length of the house. He took a moment to examine himself in the ornately carved gold-framed mirror before bothering to answer it. Even though he was about to turn forty, he had to admit, he was a good-looking man. The few flecks of gray in his otherwise black hair made him appear distinguished rather than old, or so he had been told, and his athletic physique added to his youthful appearance.

Carlos took out his phone and put it to his ear while turning his head back and forth to look at himself from different angles in the mirror. He twisted at the waist, admiring the thick, gold necklace glimmering in the soft light.

"*Hola.*" He took a step closer and smiled, examining his straight, white teeth.

"We lost her."

He pressed the phone closer to his ear. "Excuse me?" he spat in Spanish.

"We lost her...at a rest stop." Pedro began to ramble in his native tongue. "She went to the bathroom with Maria. We never saw her come out."

"How do you *lose* someone you are being paid to deliver to me?" Carlos did not yell, but his voice trembled with rage. The anger was palpable, and his choice of words made it obvious that he would hold his employees accountable. In Carlos's world, that was not a good thing.

"We are looking—"

Carlos did not give him time to respond. "Find her," he said. "Or I will find *you.*"

No more words were necessary. He continued to the back of the house, his shoes making a sharp, clicking noise as they hit the tiled floor, providing an indication of his anger to all of the staff. Flinging open the door of his office and slamming it closed behind him, he paced in front of his desk for a few moments, muttering to himself.

Memories of the first time he'd smuggled drugs came flooding back to him as the enormity of this failure sank in.

It had all been arranged. All he had to do was drive down to Mexico and pick up the cargo. Adrenaline and a touch of fear flowed through him again just by thinking about it. He could almost see those flashing red lights reflecting off the walls as they had done in his rearview mirror that night. His first time smuggling had resulted in an eight-year sentence in a federal prison. He had thought his life was over.

But he'd put those years to good use, taking advantage of the adult education programs provided, as well as making contacts and forming networks. There was no place better for forging lifelong friendships and setting up pacts than a penitentiary. Over those years, he had accrued respect and admiration from those who held power, and soon learned that the four years he served in a federal pen became a respected calling card outside the wire fence.

As soon as he was released for good behavior, he'd started a roofing company, but that was a front for what he was actually doing—laying the groundwork for his drug business. He would never do the job of transporting drugs himself again...he had learned his lesson. He would pay others to do it. That's where the money was.

Carlos had been twenty-three at the time. Getting caught was the lowest he had ever felt, but he had risen from the ashes to create a narcotics empire of enormous reach, one that placed him in the ranks of the top drug lords in all of Mexico—and the world.

He would not allow this current dilemma to defeat him either. He would find a way around it, through it. He would rise again, just as he'd surmounted his impoverished beginnings and jail sentence.

But Carlos knew he had to react quickly before the authorities discovered the elusive Mrs. Madison was no longer in his custody—and before she showed up somewhere alive and well. Being a businessman accustomed to setbacks, it did not take Carlos long to decide on his course of action. He reached for his phone just as someone knocked timidly on the door.

"A package for you, *señor.*"

Carlos walked to the door and opened it to find a young man, one of his newest employees, holding a small box in his hands. "You said you wished to know as soon as it arrived."

A slow smile spread across Carlos's face as he realized the value of this gift and its timing. It had to be a sign that God was on his side. "Yes. I have been waiting."

After dismissing the courier and tearing open the overnight express package, he stared at the phone in his hands with a large smile on his face. It didn't take long to find the contact he was seeking and tap the number. The call was answered on the very first ring.

Chapter 18

"Cait? Is that you? Are you okay?"

"Sorry to disappoint you, *amigo*."

Carlos waited for his words to sink in. He heard a sigh—almost a groan—of disappointment and anger, and could envision the torture on Blake Madison's face when he realized his wife's phone was now in the hands of her kidnapper. It would be logical for him to assume that she was as well, which made him doubly glad he had instructed Pedro to ship the phone to him.

"What do you want, Carlos? Where's Cait?"

"*Señor* Madison, I have an offer for you."

"If it involves releasing my wife, I'm listening."

Carlos had been told when you smile on the phone, it makes you sound more sincere, so that is what he did. "Yes, *amigo*. I have had a change of heart. I will accept your offer."

"What offer is that?"

"You for your wife."

"Why?"

"Because I have decided it is not fair. She did not kill my son. You did."

A loud exhalation of air was followed by, "When and where?"

"I have a small ranch house on the Mexican border near

Columbus, New Mexico."

He heard Madison cover the phone and a muffled conversation as he talked to his partner.

They are falling for it. I may have lost her, but I will still get Madison.

Carlos heard Blake come back on the line. "We'll need Proof of Life first."

Now it was Carlos who exhaled. They had not fallen for his ruse so easily, after all—yet he knew he still held all the cards. "I do not have time for such games. Your wife is alive and well. You can take the offer or leave it." Carlos was no longer smiling as he heard more rustling of the phone and whispering.

"Let me talk to her."

He ignored the request. "Nine o'clock tomorrow morning. Sharp. I do not tolerate tardiness. Any failure to follow my directions will cause the death of your wife."

"I need to talk to her first." Blake's voice was strong and in control. "*Now.*"

Carlos's heart raced. He was losing control of the situation. "*Señor*, I am being merciful, and yet you are causing me to change my mind!"

"Calm down, Carlos." Now it was Madison's voice that wavered a little. "We're at least eight hours from there. What's the address?"

"There's no address." Carlos gave the directions. "No cops. Just you. Or she dies. Understand?"

"Okay, but tell Cait—"

Carlos hung up the phone and laughed loud enough to

be heard throughout the house. He had told Madison not tell the police, but he wasn't going to let this opportunity go by without getting as many law enforcement officials—and maybe even some media—involved as possible. He had set the time for the meeting at nine o'clock the next morning, so he still had plenty of time to leak the information and prepare the site.

Maybe I'll throw a couple of other roadblocks in just to raise the stakes.

He leaned back in his plush leather chair with his hands clasped behind his head and smiled. If Blake's wife surfaced before tonight, he would track her down and kill her—or if possible, re-capture her and continue with his original plan. In that case, he would unite Blake and his wife, but not here on Earth. It wasn't the way he had planned things, but the end result was satisfactory. His only regret was not being able to see Blake Madison's face when the pieces all came together.

Colt looked over at Blake. "He's baiting you, trying to get under your skin. Don't let him win."

Blake nodded but otherwise made no comment. He stared straight ahead, his eyes dull and despairing with a look that conveyed he was seeing things that weren't really there. His hand came up slowly to his chest as if to put his heart back in its rightful place—or perhaps make sure it was still there.

"Something must have happened—"

"Or it's part of the plan." Blake looked at him for the first time. "Get my hopes up and then dash them."

Colt frowned. He didn't want to admit it, but Blake could

be right. "Like I said before, we can't be thinking about what might be happening. Let's just stick to the facts."

"I really don't need a pep talk right now, Colt." Blake turned his face toward the window, and Colt knew it was time to shut up. Blake wanted time to sort things out.

Colt looked out his window, and his own thoughts began to wander. He didn't want to think about the time when his own heart had broken, but lack of conversation and the steady whir of the road led his thoughts there anyway.

He smelled the smoke. Tasted it. Felt the kick of his gun each time he pulled the trigger and knew he was hitting his targets. But after the last RPG ripped through the wall a few feet away, it was like a giant hand had reached down and snuffed out all sound.

Damn Pentagon pansies. Griff had told them the guy was lying when he'd said the compound was not well defended. But they'd gone ahead and sent the cavalry in to rescue the hostages anyway. As a result, they'd gotten pounded from every direction.

Colt breathed a sigh of relief when he sighted Griff, alive and well, and in an animated discussion with a group of female hostages. He was glad she was in the large holding room, safe from all the shit going on outside. It had been one hell of a firefight out there to get control of the facility and sort out the bad guys.

When they got back to camp, they'd have a good time swapping stories.

Chapter 19

At last, Cait could take it no longer. The room was quiet—had been for quite some time. As quietly as she could, she opened the stall door, holding her breath and teetering on one foot as she leaned out. She heard voices outside, but it was no different than the constant hum of the rest stop.

Taking a deep breath, she walked to the sink, her gaze intent on the mirrors that would warn her of anyone entering. Seeing no one, she turned on the tap and leaned down, almost groaning in eagerness as she cupped her hands and drank thirstily. The water was lukewarm and smelled strongly of chlorine, but she had never tasted anything so delicious.

When she was satisfied, she looked around, hoping someone had inadvertently left a lipstick or eyeliner behind. Seeing nothing, she knew she had to improvise. She felt a strange sense of peace, even though she knew she was not yet out of danger. The thought of walking out the door and running into Pedro or Juan sent a shiver of fear down her spine and quickly dispelled the sense of elation she felt at being free from the bathroom stall. She gazed wistfully at the door before turning her attention back to the sink.

Bending over and splashing her face again, she relished how good the simple act felt. It revived her enough to think perhaps she could approach someone for help. Just the thought of that made her heart practically burst. She would ask to borrow a phone and call Blake. She would hear his voice. She would see him soon!

In the midst of her reverie, she felt rather than heard someone come into the room from behind her. She continued splashing her face, thinking they would go into a stall, but when she didn't hear a door close, she lifted her gaze to the mirror.

Water continued dripping from her face and hands, but her heart and her breathing stopped.

Maria stood behind her, staring at her as if she were a ghost. "We came back for the shoes, *señora*." She pointed to the sneakers that still sat in the stall with the battered door. Cait shifted her gaze to the reflection of the shoes in the mirror, but could do little more than blink. Her eyes were the only body part that seemed to function. She could not think. Could not breathe. Of course, they could not leave evidence behind. Why had she not thought of that? The sneakers would be all the authorities would need to be hot on her trail.

When she heard heavy footsteps approaching, Cait's hands dropped to the sink to help support her. Pedro, apparently sensing that something was wrong since Maria had not returned immediately with the shoes, appeared at the door.

She saw his face in the mirror, red with fury. His eyes scanned the room and landed upon the stall where she had hidden. The *OUT OF ORDER* sign was no longer visible because the door stood open.

"*Debo matarte ahora!*" I should kill you now.

Maria grabbed his arm as Cait swung around to face him, water still dripping from her face.

"No!" Maria hissed. "You will anger Carlos even more."

A sensation of intense sickness and desolation swept over Caitlin, like icy fingers sliding across every nerve in her spine. She remained absolutely unmoving for a moment, except for the electrifying shudder that reverberated through her. Then her teeth began to chatter as she tried to suppress the overwhelming feeling of terror that consumed her.

"Carlos does not like these games." Pedro spoke in English for the first time while eyeing her with a look so full of rage and violence it made Caitlin begin to back away.

He grabbed her brutally by the arm. "Do not make a sound, or I will kill you." The blade on the knife he held made a whooshing sound as it swung open with the press of a button. "You have cost us much time."

Caitlin had never heard him speak English before. She wanted to nod but was too paralyzed with fear to move. The voices of several women reached them just as Pedro pushed her toward the door. Caitlin followed him, silent and defeated. She did not make eye contact with anyone she passed, though she could tell they were eyeing her questioningly.

Once inside the vehicle, Caitlin yielded to the compulsive sobs that shook her, but Pedro was unmoved by her anguish. He drove to a more secluded spot at the rest stop, under some trees and away from other cars. While Juan bound both her hands and her legs, Pedro sat in the front seat, muttering to himself while unlocking a small box.

Caitlin closed her eyes as tightly as she could and tried to concentrate on being anywhere but in this place. She forced herself to envision the tranquil fields of Hawthorne and her husband's sparkling blue eyes as a way to calm her mind, but the fear in her chest was so all-consuming there was no longer room for breath and air.

Pedro turned around and grabbed her shoulder, shaking

her. "Open your eyes."

He spoke in English again, which unnerved her.

"Thees is how Carlos controls hees women."

Her gaze fell on a large syringe and the amber fluid it contained.

She didn't scream, and she didn't resist. She just fainted dead away.

After making a couple of additional calls to prepare for his guests at his ranch house, Carlos went outside to the gardens for a walk. His phone rang, and seeing it was Pedro, he answered it. "Did you find her?"

"Sí. We've got her."

Carlos thought he had misheard. "Madison's wife? You got her back?"

"Sí."

"Continue with the original plan. How close are you?"

There was a long pause. "Just a few hours."

Carlos could tell something was wrong. "Then what is the matter?"

"We are back on the road. But she is sick."

"What do you mean?"

"She fainted. Gets sick all the time. Won't eat."

"I need her *alive*. Do you understand? She has not been drugged. Correct?"

"No. She has been given nothing."

"Does she need a doctor?"

There was a slight pause. "Maria says she does not need a doctor."

"How would Maria…" Carlos stopped mid-sentence as the pieces began to come together.

"Never mind. Call me when you are getting close to the ranch house."

He hung up the phone, but he was smiling again. *Could it be I get two for the price of one?*

Chapter 20

Colt pulled over at the next rest stop. He knew Blake needed to get out and decompress a little after the last phone call from Carlos. Anyway, the storm they had just driven through had worn him out. The rain had stopped now, but he needed a break.

"You hanging in there, buddy?" Colt eyed Blake with a look of concern.

"I'm good."

Colt climbed out of the truck and had just turned to push the button on the key fob to lock the doors when a woman, somewhat out of breath, approached them.

"Thanks for coming so fast. The ladies' room is right this way."

She had started to turn away but must have noticed the two men stop and look at each other in confusion. "I'm Margaret Thomas. You're the cops I called, right?" She shifted her gaze to Colt's truck with the rack of lights on top, and then back at the two men dressed in tactical cargo pants. A look of doubt spread across her face.

"Yeah. We were the closest unit." Colt spoke up while locking his gaze with Blake's and giving him a let's-go-with-it look.

"I didn't know you'd get here so quick." The woman kept

talking as she walked into the building. "Call me distrustful or prejudiced, but I'm telling you, something wasn't right."

"Maybe you should start at the beginning." Colt quickened his step to catch up to her. "Dispatch didn't tell us much."

"Okay. Well, I work at the information desk." She nodded toward the information area but kept walking. "And we heard all kinds of commotion from the ladies' restroom."

By this time, they were standing outside the door. She stuck her head in and yelled. "Anyone in here? Men coming in." When no one answered, she opened the door.

"By the time I could get away to investigate, I found this."

Colt followed her in and stared at the stall door that hung by one hinge. The huge dents near the latch revealed obvious impressions of the large boot that had kicked it in. He shifted his glance to Blake, who stood with fingers curled into fists in an obvious effort to control his emotions. His chest moved in and out with deep, slow breaths. It was the type of breathing usually seen right before stepping into the line of fire on the battlefield.

"What else did you see?"

"I saw some Hispanic males running around here like they'd lost something. That's what I saw." Margaret stood with her hands on her hips.

"How many?" Colt turned his attention back to her.

"There were two males, but then I think there was a female with them, too."

"Hispanic female?" Blake's gaze tore into her.

The woman nodded. "But I honestly didn't notice her until they came back a second time."

"They left and came back?" Colt tilted his head to make sure he'd heard correctly.

"See?" Margaret threw her hands in the air. "I thought it was pretty strange, too. Everybody told me I was crazy." She took a step closer. "But the strangest thing is, when they left the second time, there was another person with them."

Colt rubbed his chin, trying to appear calm. Blake was behind him now, near the sinks. He couldn't see him, but he had heard his breath catch in his throat. "Another female?"

Margaret nodded.

"With long, blonde hair?" Blake's voice cracked noticeably.

The woman cocked her head, her brows narrowed. "No. She had short, dark hair. Messy. Unkempt. Dirty-looking."

"Was she Hispanic?" Colt was afraid to look at Blake now. He still hadn't told him about the hair found at the hotel.

"I don't think so." Margaret shook her head. "I wasn't really close enough to see. But for some reason, I don't think so."

"Anything else you remember?"

"No. That's about it. I just thought it was all a little strange."

Colt took a step toward her and shook her hand. "Thanks for your help. This could be really important."

Margaret dug a card out of her pocket. "I'm off now, but here's my contact info in case you need to get in touch with me."

"Thanks. We're just going to take a quick look around and then we'll get out of here."

As she handed him the card, her gaze landed on the stall door at the end. "Now how did that get open," she muttered, walking over to it and closing the door. "It clearly says it's out of order."

Both men looked at the door and then at each other.

Margaret turned back to Colt. "I sure hope you figure out what happened in here. I don't know who's going to pay for that door."

"Thanks for your help. I'll give you a call if I think of any other questions."

She nodded and leaned to the side to acknowledge Blake, but her gaze turned to one of confusion and concern upon doing so. She looked back at Colt and shrugged before heading out the door.

When Colt turned around, Blake was kneeling down in front of the sinks and was holding on to the counter with his head lying against his hands.

"Buddy, what's up?" Colt walked over and put his hand on his shoulder. It crossed his mind that this was all too much for him. He was too close to this. He shouldn't have brought him along.

Slowly, Blake turned over one hand and opened it, revealing an ornate wedding band. Colt knelt down beside him. He recognized it instantly. Hell, he'd helped Blake pick out the matching engagement ring.

Blake swallowed hard, his eyes glazed and staring. "She never took it off. Not for anything."

Colt stood back up and stared into the mirrors, trying to see what Cait had seen. She'd made a conscious effort to leave the ring, hoping someone would find it and turn it in. He studied Blake and could almost read his thoughts. His wife had known she was near the Mexican border. Had known if they went across it, she might never make it back. She'd made a last-ditch effort to get away and had somehow failed, but still managed to leave her husband something tangible to hold on to.

A piece of her to remember.

Chapter 21

Colt put his hand on Blake's shoulder and gave it a squeeze. "Come on, man. We'd better get back on the road. We're close, and we've got a date with Carlos."

He was just starting to turn around when something on the mirror he'd been staring at became visible in a different angle of light. He stepped closer and moved his head back and forth, trying to get it to reappear.

"What are you doing?" Blake took a step closer and looked at the mirror, too.

"Does that look like words or something?"

Both men leaned down. "That looks like an 'N,' maybe," Blake said.

"And an 'M.'" Colt looked at Blake. "N.M. New Mexico."

The letters were barely visible, apparently written in soap that had since dried.

"Is that more letters underneath?"

Both men leaned in close again. "I think it's a 'D,' an 'A,' and an 'R.'" Colt straightened back up. "Looks like there's something after that, but it's smeared."

Blake was staring blankly at the mirror, but Colt could see he was deep in thought, trying to figure out what the message was. What had she been trying to convey? A name? A place?

"Has to be part of a license plate," Blake finally said. "Either she didn't see the whole thing, or she didn't have time to write it out."

Colt's eyes went back to the writing. That's not what he'd been thinking, but it made sense. She had limited time to convey important information, and essentially nothing to convey it with. Instead of writing HELP, or CAIT WAS HERE, she'd written down the license plate of the vehicle she was in. If they could put that out across police channels, there would be that many more eyes looking for her.

"Good thinking, brother. You're probably right." Colt started scrolling through his contacts for the man who could track down a New Mexico license plate.

He sighed loudly when his first choice didn't pick up. "Lou, it's Colt. This is urgent. Need to see if you can find anything on a plate for me. New Mexico. D A R-something or something-D A R."

He hurriedly sent a text message to Podge and then turned back to Blake, who had a slightly more hopeful look on his face. If they could find her before the exchange was to be made—all the better, because neither of them had much faith that Carlos would keep his end of the bargain.

The license plate number wasn't much, but it was more than they'd had before. It was a start.

By the time they made their way back to Colt's truck, the police that had been called arrived. Colt briefed them and called the FBI to provide the update, all the while pacing the sidewalk in front of the visitor center with his phone glued to his ear. He explained that they had a positive ID based on the description, but didn't see any need to mention the ring. He knew there was no way he would get it out of Blake's hand, and he didn't want to rip his friend's heart out by trying.

Anyway, the FBI would have access to the security video. Surely she would be on it—as well as the faces of her kidnappers.

As soon as Colt climbed back into the truck, Blake spoke. "You knew about her hair." He turned his head toward him. "That it was cut."

The words weren't said in an accusatory way, but like he was stating a fact, trying to catch up.

Colt turned the key. "Yeah, bro. I knew. Sorry."

Blake nodded and stared blankly out the window again. A muscle in his jaw clenched beneath the black stubble of his beard. His bold blue eyes were now dull orbs of pain.

"You still good to go on this?"

Blake's head jerked back, and his gaze met Colt's. "I'm good to go." But his eyes grew instantly distant and despondent again. "Even if I have to operate with no information."

Colt started to back out of the parking space. "Sorry about that."

"I'm a big boy, Colt. I've been through this shit before."

Colt was about to say, "not when it's your wife," but just nodded instead. "I didn't want you worrying about something we weren't sure was true."

"Okay. But stop it." He leveled his eyes on Colt. "I can sift through the facts as well as anyone else. It's not my first rodeo."

"Fine. I'll give you everything I've got from now on."

He glanced over at Blake. "But you've got to concentrate on those facts, not on what *might* be happening." He shook his head and tried to keep his voice from cracking. "We can't go there."

"You're worried, too." Blake stared out the window again and said the words as if he were talking to himself, just stating another simple fact. Colt didn't bother to deny it. Blake knew him too well for that.

Colt let his breath out between his teeth. "Don't worry. Cait's a strong woman. She'll hang in there."

And I'll give my last breath to put her back in your arms if that's what it takes.

Colt leaned down and turned up the radio so they could both think about something other than the present. The song playing was *The Dance* by Garth Brooks. He turned it back down.

Chapter 22

Weariness and exhaustion enveloped Colt as he tried to concentrate on the directions Carlos had given them. He was glad for the few hours of sleep he'd gotten the first night on the road because they'd been moving ever since.

They were now less than ten miles away according to his GPS. That was both good and bad news. He felt like he could relax a little because they still had time for reconnaissance, yet what they would find at the end of this journey was yet to be seen.

Out of the corner of his eye, he saw Blake stiffen even before he saw the traffic in front of him come to a sudden stop.

"What's going on?"

Colt leaned to his left but could only see the line of traffic—not what had stopped it. He kept himself from looking at his watch but glanced down to the clock on the console. Precious minutes were ticking by, bringing them closer and closer to the established time for the exchange. Carlos had been clear about his instructions. Colt's heart began to pick up its pace.

One glance at Blake and he could tell his friend was thinking the same thing. Blake's face was contorted with suppressed emotion. He looked like he was getting ready to jump out of his skin.

"It's probably just a minor accident up ahead." Colt tried to relieve Blake's worries.

"Or it's Carlos."

The thought had crossed Colt's mind, but he'd instantly discounted it. Hearing Blake say the words made him re-think the possibility. Maybe Carlos hadn't had a change of heart at all. Maybe he had no intention of doing the exchange. It could be he'd thought of another way to torture Blake—by causing him to sit in traffic and make him late, thereby shifting the blame to Blake for the exchange not being made. Could he be that cruel?

Colt's mind kicked into overdrive. Carlos had made the call about the exchange about the same time Caitlin had probably been trying to escape. Perhaps he'd been alerted to her disappearance and had been trying to salvage something out of his plan.

He glanced over at Blake. Be that as it may, the man beside him was going to show up at the designated place at the designated time even if he had to hoof it the rest of the way. There would be no stopping him.

After a few agonizing minutes, the line of vehicles started moving again, giving Colt a view of what had brought traffic to a halt. A single truck with a flashing yellow light sat on the side of the road. When Colt's truck was the next in line to pass, a Hispanic man with a flag stepped onto the road and flagged him to a halt.

"Don't stop." Blake leaned forward and slammed the dashboard with his fists. "Keep going. Hit him if you have to."

Colt brought the truck to a stop. "I can't just hit him, bro."

"It's one of Carlos's men." Blake's voice was husky with weariness and the impossible hours they'd been keeping. "He planned this."

"We don't know that." Colt unbuckled his seatbelt. "Don't move. I'm going to have a little chat with this guy."

He jumped out of the truck and strode toward the lone figure, his hands curled into fists.

The man looked startled when he noticed Colt exiting the truck, and petrified when he saw the look on his face.

"What's the holdup?" Colt stormed over to him. "Why did you stop us?"

Traffic continued moving in the other direction with drivers slowing down to watch the unfolding scene occurring in the opposite lane.

"*Amigo*, you must get back in your truck."

"I'm not your *amigo*." Colt's voice rose above the sound of the cars passing by. "Step aside or I will run you down."

"No, *señor*. You must wait."

"Wait for what?"

The man pulled a phone out of his pocket and hit a button as if he were receiving a call. "*Sí. Sí.*"

He looked at Colt. "You can move now, *señor*."

Colt stared at him a little longer, trying to decide whether to punch him or get back in the truck.

Blake decided for him, yelling from the truck in a loud, anxious voice, "Let's go!"

"Remember my face." Colt grabbed the man by his shirt collar and leaned down so his face was just inches from the man's. "If you ever see me again, you'd better run for your life."

The man did not acknowledge that he'd heard except for taking a step back off to the side of the road when Colt released him. He gave the flag a half-hearted shake to show the lane was now open.

When Colt crawled back in the truck, Blake was breathing hard, as if just sitting there watching what had taken place had physically winded him. "Put the hammer down," was all he said. "We need to make up for lost time."

"I'm on it." Colt stomped on the gas and threw gears until they were once again flying across the wide-open road.

When they were about two miles away from the meeting point, Colt deliberately ignored the turn onto the narrow road that Carlos had listed in his directions. They needed to get the lay of the land first. They still had ten minutes to spare before they were supposed to arrive, and Colt had no idea if Cait was actually in the house—or alive for that matter.

Blake must have been thinking the same thing. "Pull over."

Colt pulled into the parking lot of long-abandoned adobe-style structure, but the house number was still on the door. He pulled out his laptop and went to work. "I'll bring that address up on Google maps, and we'll go from there."

As he tapped on keys, Blake leaned over and looked at the screen. "Where in the hell are we?"

"Looks like we're right in the middle," he murmured, staring at the screen.

"Middle of what?" Blake bent down to get a closer look.

"Fucking nowhere." Colt zoomed out until they saw the

road where they were supposed to have turned. They both studied the narrow dirt lane. "Looks like one way in and one way out."

"Like Iraq." Blake studied the screen. "They funnel you in for an ambush."

Colt continued to move the mouse in a wider circle around the area. "Perfect place for a trap for sure." He looked at his watch. "We have a drone coming. Should be overhead soon."

Blake nodded toward his right. "We need a sniper or two on that hill for overwatch."

"Podge has two on the move in this direction but no ETA yet."

Blake leaned closer, scrutinizing the picture on the computer screen. "Zoom in on the house."

They both studied the image of a dilapidated ranch structure that sat on the hill above them. "Doesn't exactly look like the standard of living Carlos Valdez is accustomed to."

"Definitely not. This is probably just one of his drug lairs where he loads up and drops off supplies."

As Blake stared at the house, his jaw tightened, and he winced. Colt knew what he was thinking. It was no place for someone like his wife to be. Three days ago, they'd been going about their business, their biggest worry being what to do for their anniversary. Now, she was in the hands of the most infamous and dangerous drug lord on the planet, probably fighting for her life. The world was upside down.

"Nothing about this makes sense."

Colt nodded to his left at a rickety chain-link fence that ran as far as the eye could see. "Except that right there is the

Mexican border." A small sign, hanging crooked on the fence read: *Boundary of the United States of America.*

Yeah. Just close enough for Carlos to scurry back to his rat hole if things get hot."

Blake leaned back and ran his hand through his hair. "I'd like to get closer. Take a look around."

Just then, Colt's phone rang. He answered and said, "Copy that. You have a TOT?" He hung up and turned to Blake. "Time on Target for the drone is six minutes. We'll get the images up before we go in."

"Perfect." He looked at his watch. "You're a miracle worker, you know that? Pulling a damn drone out of your ass like that."

"It's your company. Your contacts. We have sub-contractors all over the country."

Blake turned to him. "You're the one with friends in high places."

"He hasn't even been briefed on this yet," Colt replied, referring to the President. "This is all Phantom Force."

Colt had put a bug in President Calloway's ear about the need for specialized units that could respond anywhere in the world on short notice, and had even provided him a copy of Phantom Force Tactical's business plan. The President was one of the few people that knew Colt's true passion was to create a Shadow Warrior Assault Team or SWAT, a specialized force capable of responding to situations and performing counter-terrorism measures all over the world.

For the most part, the organization would stay in the background, only getting involved when other more routine methods failed to produce results. But the company would be a true amalgamation of special operators from all military branches, offering a wide array of specialties. The Specialized Assault Squads (SAS) could spin up and be ready to deploy within hours, making it the most seasoned, potent, mobile fighting force in action.

Right now, it was just a concept on paper, but Colt knew it could work. Unconventional warfare required swift reaction and an unconventional chain of command. Instead of having information filter down through dozens of agencies and individuals, SWAT would simply get their orders from the President or the Secretary of Defense—and then it would be game on.

For now, they were getting into the business with the umbrella organization of Phantom Force Tactical. While Blake ran most of the day-to-day logistics of hiring, training, and negotiating contracts, Colt was happy to be part of the boots on the ground. Even though he had just turned forty, he was still comfortable conducting high-risk missions deep within enemy territory. Having to make decisions based on an analysis of what was happening on the ground—mostly in situations where it was impossible to consult higher command—had become second nature to him. The ability to be fully operational even when detached from a command structure was what made him such an asset wherever he went.

Colt's decisions were instinctive because they were based on experience...and audacity. Some might say he had a healthy dose of luck mixed in, but anyone who had seen him in action understood that his 'luck' came more from fortitude and determination—not a special nod from the Universe.

The President knew it, and so did just about every national security agency in DC. They relied on him as a consultant and security asset, yet Colt was able to keep a low profile—almost a cloak of invisibility. No one—not even Blake—knew who he was 'freelancing' with sometimes.

"Yeah. Well, you're good at smooth-talking them into showing up on short notice."

"I think everyone agrees it's a pretty good cause. A lot of people know Cait—"

Colt stopped himself and shook his head. It was impossible to talk about. He didn't want Blake thinking about what the stakes in this game were. *He* didn't want to think about them either. Blake's life for hers was the worst-case scenario. But Colt knew they both planned on finding a way to swap Carlos's life for both of theirs…and rid the world of an element of evil so that it could never return to cause this type of pain and misery ever again.

Both men began getting their equipment together. Blake would be unarmed except for a knife hidden in a sheath under his pants leg and a small camera in a pen in his shirt. The command post would relay what they were seeing about numbers and the location of Cait into the earpieces of Colt and the snipers.

Everyone knew Blake would be searched and would be in great danger if or when they discovered the device, but they would have eyes and ears on the situation for that much longer—and Blake was pretty experienced at taking care of himself. No one had any doubt he could handle the situation—the only question mark was Cait.

The federal agencies involved in the case had been *officially* briefed on a limited basis, but Colt wanted as few people as possible informed about the actual exchange. He didn't want decisions made based on committee, which was what invariably happened when the government got involved.

Colt slipped on his vest and loaded it with fresh magazines. Then he leaned back against the truck and crossed his arms. "Don't screw this up, bro."

Blake cocked his head. "What's your definition of screw up?"

"Get yourself killed."

He shrugged. "It's a dangerous mission."

"But the reward is worth it."

A smile crept into Blake's expression. "Yeah, brother. Copy that."

Colt had never met anyone comparable to Blake's valor and conduct in battle. It was not a whim or foolish passion for him, it was a serious choice. A strange choice perhaps because he was one of the most compassionate and gentle men Colt had ever met.

"You good?" Blake's tone was even and controlled. His unreadable expression and relaxed demeanor revealed little of his mood, but Colt knew the pressure he was under.

Colt looked up from the suppressor he was screwing onto his rifle. "You have to ask?" He removed the grin from his face as he stared into Blake's eyes. "How about you?"

"I'm good."

Chapter 23

The men's attention was suddenly drawn to a moving dust trail on the road above them, heading toward the house. Colt began tapping away on the keys of his computer, trying to find the uplink for the drone footage. It came online just as the vehicle came to an abrupt halt by a side porch.

Both of them leaned in, breathless, as the occupants of the van began to exit the vehicle. Two Hispanic males got out of the front seats, and both turned and opened the back doors. A short Hispanic woman stepped out of the passenger side, and then one of the men leaned in with what appeared to be a knife. After a few moments, a figure wearing an oversized black sweatshirt with the hood up was pulled from behind the driver's side.

Both Colt and Blake knew it was Cait, but neither of them said anything. Neither even breathed until she had disappeared. When Colt glanced over at Blake, he was staring up at the house, his blue eyes scanning the terrain, obviously analyzing and assessing the possibility—or the probability—that Carlos would not hold up his end of the bargain, and figuring out the desperate measures he would be required to take to change that scenario. Colt's phone dinged just then and he gazed down at the screen. "We've got two snipers up above the house looking for a sweet spot."

Blake's head swiveled, and he twisted to get a better view of the hilltop. They should be able to find something up there.

Colt leaned back over the computer to look at the images the drone was sending. "Strange, they don't have any guards or a perimeter set up that I can see." He gazed up at Blake. "Do you think Carlos is that sure of himself? Do you think he's even in there?"

"It doesn't add up. I've always heard Carlos is overly cautious. Bodyguards. Dogs. The whole nine yards. That's how he got to be as powerful as he is."

"Wish we had more guys on our side, but we'll make it work." Colt bent back over the computer screen and pointed. "I'm going to go back and drive up the road about a mile, then get out. As you drive the rest of the way in, I'll be making my way up this hill and should hit the crest about the same time as you get to the house. You'll have the snipers on one side and me on the other."

Blake nodded. "Sounds good. That's my preferred route for extraction, too."

Colt's phone rang, and for the first time, Blake didn't ask him to put it on speaker. He just turned his head toward the window.

"Looks like we're ready on this end," Podge said. "You guys good?"

"We're good." Colt turned his head toward Blake. "You're good. Right?"

Blake just nodded. "Got my BFK. I'm good."

Colt reported back to Podge. "Blake's good to go. He's got his Big Fucking Knife with him."

"Sounds like something you'd do, Colt. Take a knife into a gunfight."

Colt laughed. "Hell, yeah. Gotta keep things interesting."

Podge got serious. "You guys better stop goofing around. You're about to get into some heavy-duty shit."

"Roger that." Colt became all business again. "We saw two Hispanic males and a female go into the house with Caitlin. No idea how many more are waiting inside."

The phone line went silent for a moment. "How are you feeling about this, Colt? What's the trigger to call this thing off?"

Again, Colt looked at Blake. It was clear there was only one way this was going to end—and it involved gunfire. "We're going in," was all he said.

After he'd hung up the phone, he exhaled. "Podge has everything ready on their end."

Blake nodded.

"And he told me to tell you, 'if you can't be safe...'"

A grim smile lit Blake's face as he finished the sentence. "Be deadly."

Colt knew Blake could take care of himself, but he did have one concern. If Blake lived and Caitlin died, a single bullet was going to come precariously close to extinguishing two lives.

Blake looked at his watch. "Looks like it's show time. You ready?"

"I'm ready if you're ready." Colt noticed that Blake was deceptively calm, except for the leg that still bounced.

The two of them shook off the danger and the pressure with a fist bump and a grin. "Let's do this."

Colt turned the truck around and went back to the dirt road that led to the house. He turned in and then pulled to the side and stopped the vehicle.

"What's up, dude?" Blake looked over at him with a confused expression. "It's time."

"I know, but my gut's telling me this isn't right."

Just then, two marked police cars came racing up the road past them with sirens blaring, followed by another three vehicles with flashing lights.

"What the hell is that about?" Both men leaned forward, waving their hands for them to stop, but they were gone. Colt put his foot on the gas pedal and barreled toward the house.

Blake's face had turned white. "Carlos will think we called for backup," he said, stating the obvious.

This was exactly why Colt had kept the time of the meeting from the federal agencies. He knew they would try to outdo one another by being the first on the scene. These vehicles, however, appeared to be from local and state agencies. Someone else had tipped them off.

Carlos?

Colt had the gas pedal pressed to the floor, causing the truck's suspension to groan and whine over every pothole. They had just crested the last rise before the house and saw that the cars had fanned out in front of the building. Officers were opening their doors and taking up positions behind them with guns drawn.

Blake unclicked his seatbelt and had his door open even though the truck was still moving at a high rate of speed.

"Hold on, bro. Let me get a little closer." Colt reached out and grabbed Blake's arm to keep him from jumping out of the moving truck. "I still don't like the looks of this."

"Just get as close as you can," Blake hissed through clenched teeth, one leg hanging out of the door. "I've got to stop them and get into the house."

Blake had one foot on the ground by the time Colt brought the truck to a complete stop behind two cruisers. "Hold on a minute, damn it." Colt grabbed Blake's arm and gave it a yank before he could get the whole way out.

That was the last thing he remembered before an ear-splitting explosion shook the ground and the truck, sending fragments of boards and nails and glass showering onto the windshield and hood.

Chapter 24

Cait felt numb as they cut the zip ties from her wrists and ankles and pulled her out of the van in front of a forlorn-looking house. Was this where she was going to meet Carlos? She gazed at it from beneath the hood of the sweatshirt they had made her wear.

Her mind flitted back to the house in Virginia, to the kids, to her husband. Was he looking for her right now? Had he found her? She glanced over her shoulder before she went through the door, and imagined him watching from some far-off hill. The thought brought such peace that she almost smiled.

But then she felt the cold steel of a gun against her back as Pedro pushed her through the doorway. His urgency, and the fact that he had exchanged his knife for a gun, replaced her sense of peace with one of foreboding and fear.

Once inside, Caitlin thought she'd be taken to a room and locked inside, but that was not the case. Maria took her hand and led her swiftly to a door. "Hurry, *señora.*"

"Why?" Caitlin looked warily at the men right behind her. One of them was on his phone. "What is the hurry?"

Maria opened the door and pushed her toward the threshold. "Just hurry. *Movimiento.*"

Caitlin stopped as soon as she caught a whiff of the dank,

stale air of a cellar, and saw that the steps led down into a dark hole. She held onto the doorway. "No."

"Go," Maria hissed from behind. "You must go."

Cait stifled the whimper that almost rose in her throat. Were they putting her into some type of dungeon? All she could smell was dirt and earth. She had a sudden fear she would never see the sun again. That she was descending into her own grave.

With the men pushing her from behind, she had no choice but to descend the stairs. One of the men must have hit a light switch because the area in front of her was suddenly illuminated, and she saw she was entering a tunnel.

"Hurry. Hurry." Maria continued to push her forward with an urgency that could be felt.

Blake must be closing in—or the authorities. They are definitely in a hurry. She looked around as the men continued to herd them forward. One of them was still on the phone as if getting a progress report from someone—or giving one. His face seemed intent, and he appeared anxious to get far away from the front of the house.

Then, without warning, both of the men slowed and turned to close a large steel door Caitlin had not even noticed.

All of the light disappeared when the door closed with a deep bang that reverberated for a few moments through the shaft. Caitlin heard Pedro and Juan struggling to slide a huge steel crossbeam into place, apparently to barricade the door. *From what? From whom?*

She heard Pedro say, "*Sí*, Carlos. We are ready." A moment later, Maria's hand reached out in the darkness and held onto hers. "I'm sorry about your husband," she whispered, just before a large explosion nearly knocked Caitlin off her feet. With her ears ringing from the tremendous din, it took her a moment to process what Maria had said.

Blake had been out there. She had known it. She had felt it. And she had helped lead him into a trap.

She heard the soft click of a switch, and the tunnel became filled with dim, dusty light. Cait's eyes darted to the two men for confirmation of what had just occurred. There was no jubilation, and there was no regret. They turned around and continued through the tunnel as if they had just completed a small, irrelevant task they had been paid to do.

Her confused gaze went from their blank expressions to the remorseful one of Maria, causing a wail of grief and misery to rise of its own accord from her throat. In the same instant, her legs gave out, and she fell to her knees in anguished, uncontrollable torment. She held both hands to her face, covering her eyes as if that would stop the images that appeared before her. Even though her mind was unwilling to accept the horrific reality, her body had already acknowledged the truth.

Noooooo!

Weak and distraught, she fell forward to the cool dirt floor, her last conscious thought focused on the image of her strong husband as she had last seen him. She sucked in one more ragged breath of dusty air before succumbing to the darkness that overpowered her.

Chapter 25

Both men dove to the floor of the truck as debris pinged off the fortified windshield. Fragments continued to rain down on them, but neither of them hesitated. They immediately left the safety of the cab and ran toward the devastation, looking for survivors in the debris.

The heavy soot blinded them, and the thick smoke choked them, but it didn't take long to see that there was nothing left of the house but splinters of wood and flattened rubble. Dazed police officers with blackened faces and shell-shocked expressions wandered around, helping the injured away from the carnage. It looked like those who had remained in their cars were merely stunned, but two officers who had been close to the house were down and seriously injured—if not dead.

Colt walked up to Blake and put his arm over his shoulders. "Come on, man. They have this under control." He feared what else they might come across if they continued their search. Already, the sirens of ambulances could be heard in the distance. There was nothing more for them to do here.

Blake stood unmoving, his eyes dull and staring as he gazed at the wreckage. Colt watched as the stunned look on his face was chased away by complete disbelief, and then by an expression that disclosed he doubted the reality of what he was seeing. The look on his face was too distressing for description.

"Come on." Colt wanted to get him away from the scene, but Blake wouldn't move. Colt could almost see the wheels turning in his head. Wheels of denial. Wheels of regret.

"He wouldn't just kill her..." His voice broke off in mid-sentence.

"He would. You know he would." Colt grabbed his shoulder and shook him. "He wanted you to see it. Or more than likely, be in it. Let's go."

Blake remained where he stood, but his head slowly turned to the left, toward the fence, toward Mexico. Then he ran back to the truck.

"What are you doing?" Colt grabbed him by the shoulder. This was the outcome that Colt had dreaded the most. Not only would they not being going home with Caitlin, but Blake had been a spectator to her death—and had been mere feet from being able to save her.

"I'm getting kitted up." Blake grabbed gear out of the back of the truck, including his body armor, pistol, M-4 and extra ammo.

"For what?"

"I'm going to Mexico." Blake nodded toward the fence and the large house that could barely be seen in the distance. "There's a tunnel. She's in Mexico."

Colt scanned the distance and nodded. It made sense. Carlos was well known for his elaborate and sophisticated network of tunnels for drug smuggling. This house was situated perfectly for such an operation. Secluded. On a small rise where scouts could see for miles. Colt glanced over at Blake's intense, determined look. He knew there was no way he was going to stop him.

"Whoa. Whoa. We're not going to launch a major operation on foreign soil without the President's approval."

"It's not a major operation." Blake slammed a fresh magazine into his gun. "It's a surgical strike. Explain that to your buddy, the President."

Colt grabbed his arm. "Here's the deal. We're going to slow down. Take a deep breath."

Blake's jaw stiffened in defiance, but he stopped what he was doing and seemed willing to at least hear more.

"We're going to regroup. Get more assets on the ground. Work with whatever local force is still capable of fighting. He's thinking we're going to go home. We'll hit him tonight. With Phantom Force."

Blake took in what Colt said, his eyes roaming the area. He nodded without saying a word.

"Even with the element of surprise, there's going to be a firefight." Colt continued talking in a firm, straightforward voice that showed he was in command. "We're looking at AKs and grenades at the very least. I wouldn't rule out mortars and RPGs."

Again, Blake nodded, apparently not trusting himself to speak.

"I'm going to make some calls and organize whatever force I can. We'll pull guys from everywhere we can find them and use all of the assets we have available. You get on the phone with Brody and see if he can give us some recon on what we're going up against. Hopefully, we can organize a Joint Assault Group (JAG) in the next few hours."

Blake climbed into the passenger side of the truck with a determined look on his face. Colt shot him one last worried look and pulled out his phone. He had work to do. They were about to launch an operation on foreign soil that could have international ramifications. The President would never forgive him if he did it without telling him, yet Colt hesitated, afraid the Commander in Chief would try to stop him.

One last look at Blake made up his mind. Blake and Cait were like family. He would kill for them—and, if necessary, die for them. The President was just going to have to understand. That's just the way it had to be. He would go to the White House when this was over and ask for forgiveness—but he wasn't going to ask for permission.

Chapter 26

Cait opened her eyes and then closed them again when the light from the room blinded her. She lifted her lids again, slower this time, and saw that the sunlight was coming from a large, sliding glass door near where she was lying. With difficulty, she struggled back to consciousness, her mind for some reason resisting all efforts to comply. The first thing she noticed was that the bed she rested on was soft and comfortable, a far cry from what she had endured the last few days.

"Are you awake?"

Turning her head toward the voice, Cait saw Maria standing over her. She shifted her gaze to the ceiling and did not answer, still grappling with gaps in her memory.

"You will feel better after a warm bath." Maria pulled away the blanket that covered her. "Come, I will show you."

"Is he dead?" It all came back to her in one all-consuming wave of emotion.

Maria froze in place. "I do not know, *señora*."

"But he was there." Caitlin felt a tear slide down her cheek as all of her confusion and yearning wielded together in one upsurge of devouring heartache and loneliness.

"*Sí*." Maria bit her lip and nodded. "I think so."

When she did not move, Maria leaned over her and talked

in a whispered voice. "He will kill you. Come."

"Good." Cait did not move. She had hoped she would never wake again. There was nothing Carlos could do to her now that would hurt any worse than what he'd already done. Her heart was irreparably broken, and the shards would forever pierce her soul.

Cait closed her eyes and prayed the men from Phantom Force would not make a rescue attempt. If she were now in Mexico, which she assumed she was, their hands would be tied. Crossing an international border would not stop men like Blake's partner Nick Colton, but others—more level-headed individuals—would no doubt try to rein him in. She hoped he would listen. She didn't want to be the cause of any more bloodshed.

"Think of the children."

Cait's eyes opened in a flash. "What do you mean? You said they were safe."

"They can never be safe from Carlos." Maria looked scared. "You must do as he says. *Always.* You do not understand the power he holds."

Caitlin closed her eyes and could not suppress the soft groan that escaped her. With Blake gone and their mother in jail from a political scandal, the children's lives would be in limbo.

"Why do you do this, Maria?" She kept her eyes closed and waited for an answer. When none came, she opened them again.

Maria sat beside the bed, her eyes glistening with tears. "I do not wish to," she finally said.

Caitlin reached out for her hand. "Then why?"

Maria bit her lip as if trying to decide how much to say. "Do you have any children?"

She nodded. "*Sí*. Do not ask questions."

"I'm not afraid of Carlos," Caitlin said defiantly.

"Oh, *sí, sí*. You must be afraid." Maria practically cried. "If he cannot hurt you, he will hurt the ones you love."

"Carlos has threatened you?"

Maria nodded as a tear let loose. "He killed my husband and then my parents. He said they were not cooperating with the organization." She took a deep sobbing breath. "He will kill my son if I do not do as he says."

Caitlin allowed the words to sink in and thought about how terrified Maria must be every moment, afraid of taking a wrong step and being the cause of her son's death.

Not wanting to cause the woman any further pain, Caitlin started to sit up but laid back down as a feeling of nausea washed over her. Maria must have sensed her need. She grabbed a small wastebasket as Cait heaved through another bout of morning sickness.

"You must think of your own child." The voice was soft. Compassionate. "Do as he says."

Cait's eyes darted up to Maria, but she did not acknowledge the comment. She would play along—for now. For the baby's sake. But she would never give in or give up.

Clammy and shivering, Cait climbed from the bed and followed Maria into a bathroom that made her stop and stare. Larger than most bedrooms, it had white marble floors and ceilings ornately inlaid with gold. A spa tub sat on a platform between two pillars, its sides reflecting the soft glow of a can-dle chandelier above. In fact, there were candles burning everywhere, emitting the relaxing, soothing scent of exotic flowers.

"Come." Maria interrupted her thoughts. She handed Caitlin a plush robe and turned her back. "Give me your clothes."

Caitlin wanted nothing to do with Carlos but consented to Maria's commands. Once Maria had left the room, Cait lowered herself into the hot tub and looked at the mixture of expensive bath products within her reach. She put her head back and closed her eyes, the warm water helping her to relax and clear her mind, but no amount of scented body wash could make her feel clean from the filth she had been exposed to in the last three days.

When she was done, she dried off, wrapped herself in the robe, and stepped back into the bedroom.

Maria sat on a chair beside the sliding door that opened onto the sunlit balcony. Drawn by the soothing sound of water, Caitlin walked to the open door and stared at the landscape. The room overlooked a sparkling oval-shaped pool with an ornate fountain in the middle from which water trickled down three levels. She wondered if anyone ever swam in it or if it was just for decoration.

Her gaze continued to wander over the beautiful grounds and gardens. All around her, and growing up on each side of the balcony on trellises, were semitropical flowers and foliage, including hibiscus and orchids. She took a deep breath, inhaling their luscious fragrance.

"It is beautiful here, *señora*. You will grow to like it."

Caitlin whirled around to face her. "I'm not *staying*."

Maria shook her head. "That will be up to Carlos."

Caitlin was just about to say, "no, that will be up to my husband," when she remembered the explosion. Before she had time to stop them, tears began running down her face.

"You must forget the past," Maria said soothingly. "This is your life now."

A single knock on the door interrupted them as a young brown-skinned boy pushed in a cart of food. There was juice, fresh fruit, and elegant-looking tea sandwiches cut into neat little squares. "Some food for you, *señora*," he said without making eye contact.

Caitlin turned away but heard Maria telling the boy to leave. She poured Caitlin a glass of juice and fixed her a plate of fruit. "You must put something in your stomach if you want to stay strong."

Caitlin sat down on the bed and gazed around the room. The white gauze curtains swayed gently in the breeze, and the large windows let in warming natural light. On the far side of the room a plasma television hung by a couch, and large paintings in golden frames were scattered on the remaining walls.

Maria went to a closet and opened the door. "There are clothes for you in here. Size six."

Caitlin walked over to the closet and fingered the expensive-looking clothes. There were dresses and skirts, Armani suits, and formal gowns, as well as high heels and sandals.

She turned to Maria. "How did you know what size I wear?"

Maria shrugged. "Like I have told you, Carlos knows everything."

Caitlin went back to the balcony and stared out over the lawn. She felt like she was in an upscale resort, the kind she had read about but never visited—until she caught sight of the men carrying automatic weapons walking in the expansive yard, and others who stood at the far gate with large dogs. Farther beyond, she could see four-wheelers carrying armed men patrolling the perimeter.

Her gaze drifted back to the men by the pool. They were mostly young and looked innocent enough—until she saw the savage expression in their eyes when they looked up. Their grim faces and intense gazes spoke to a serious agenda. She knew that failure to do their duty meant a possible bullet in the head. Their lives revolved around kill or be killed.

She turned back to Maria. "Why am I here?"

"Carlos wants to meet you." She turned to the door. "Eat, *señora,* and get some rest."

Caitlin was almost sad to see Maria go. She was afraid of the woman and drawn to her at the same time. She was Cait's only connection to her past life now.

As soon as the door clicked shut, Caitlin walked over and turned the knob. It was locked. Her heart flopped and fell. As beautiful as this room was, it was to be her prison. She wondered how she was going to survive—and then tried to decide if she really wanted to.

Her hand moved to her stomach. She'd learned a lot in the fifteen years she'd worked in DC as a journalist—a lot about power, and influence, and determination. She was reminded that it was not just herself she had to worry about now. She needed to fight tooth and nail, do whatever she had to do to survive. Blake would want her to live. She was not going to die without a fight.

Caitlin sat down on the bed and felt her eyes get heavy. When she opened them again, Maria was standing by her side.

"It is time," Maria said. "Here are your clothes."

Caitlin sat up, wide awake now. "Time for what?"

"For dinner, *señora*. With Carlos. Hurry. You do not wish to be late."

Caitlin took a deep breath to prepare herself. She knew it was important for her to project an air of confidence, but she wasn't sure it was a task she was capable of accomplishing.

She stared at the long, flowing dress Maria had laid on the bed. "This is a formal affair?"

"*Sí*. You are the guest of honor."

Caitlin almost shivered at the thought. She allowed Maria to dress her but refused to look in the large mirror when she was done.

"Beautiful," Maria said when she finished fixing Cait's hair and applying makeup. "Except you need to wear a smile."

Caitlin glanced at the mirror and grimaced. Maria had evened out her hair and done a good job of styling it, but the dark color and short cut made it hard to recognize herself. She shot Maria a look of somber disgust, just as someone knocked on the door.

"It is time," Maria said again meekly.

Caitlin dug deep, fought to remain strong, and could almost hear her husband's voice sharing his military advice for getting through a tough ordeal.

Embrace the suck. She almost smiled.

Chapter 27

As Caitlin followed her guide through the large hallway, she tried to be alert, to notice everything, memorize her surroundings, and remember her way. But she had a strange feeling of detachment, as if she were watching herself from above, as if the person walking to have dinner with a drug kingpin was not really her.

Don't plan. Prepare. Don't worry. Be ready. She heard Blake's voice again, and had to suppress the urge to turn around to see if he were really there. And then, just like that, uncertainty lost its grip and fear was forgotten. She squared her shoulders raised her head, and became aware of the sound of her heels hitting the polished floor as they passed marble statues and fountains and wall upon wall of original paintings.

But it was hard not to show a look of surprise when she entered the dining room. The table was large enough to hold at least a dozen people, and was set with gold Lenox china and cut crystal stemware. Large, gold candelabras glowed, and waiters with their hands behind their backs stood along the wall, apparently ready to be of service.

Within moments, she heard voices outside the room, low-pitched but audible, and then the sound of footsteps approaching. Each *click, click, click* of shoes on the polished marble floors made her body jerk, but she willed herself to remain calm. The door on the other side of the space was opened by an unseen person, and then Carlos Valdez stepped through.

"My dear, *Señora* Madison." His movements were fluid and graceful as he strode toward her, like he'd been born into a life of royalty rather than one of poverty and crime. Dressed impeccably in white linen pants and a silk shirt, he was striking. His hair was perfect. His bright eyes aglow. Polished perfection. "Welcome to my home, my paradise."

Cait's gaze shifted to the two armed bodyguards who took positions on each side of the door, their faces emotionless, their automatic weapons draped across their chests.

Yeah. Paradise.

As Carlos drew closer with an extended hand, she saw that his tan face was crinkled with a look of welcome, but his eyes devoured her in a way that made Cait wish to flee the room. This was a man who entertained kings and presidents, lived in a world of excess and high-society friends. Yet he displayed obvious surprise when Caitlin showed no reaction to his obvious appraisal and refused to offer him her hand.

"They are not treating you well here?" he pouted. His English was flawless.

"I am here against my will." She kept her face impassive, but felt the muscles in her cheek twitch at the effort.

He laughed and waved his hand to summons one of the servers, causing the gold rings on his fingers to flash as they caught the light. "You must not think of these things tonight."

His voice sounded smooth and friendly, and he possessed a smile of imperial casualness, but Caitlin knew all of that was a mask for his evil intentions. It mattered little if he appeared angry or joyful; if he spoke kindly or harshly. He was a king here. A dictator. He reigned by force with little regard for who or what he destroyed in the process.

Caitlin studied him closely, guardedly, as he turned to give directions to a server. She wasn't sure what she had been expecting, but it wasn't this. He was clean-shaven, handsome—some might even say pretty with his flawless white teeth and easy smile—yet there was something course and rough about him.

"You expected me to have a tail, *señora?* He grinned at her. "Horns perhaps?"

The fact that he'd noticed her studying him while he was seemingly otherwise engaged reminded Caitlin that she needed to be aware of her own surroundings at all times. "I have not wasted my time thinking about what you might look like, if that is what you are asking."

She forced herself to look straight into his eyes. A spark of anger flashed there, but once again he laughed.

"I enjoy a woman with wit and cleverness. We shall get along splendidly together."

His words and his tone sent a chill up Caitlin's spine. He had a smile on his face, but the unseen energy he exuded was not positive. He seemed to be a man who only pretended to know how to show emotion or true pleasure—it did not come naturally to him.

As he pulled out her chair, his body was so close she almost trembled. Waiters began placing steaming dishes on the table, and she prayed she would not get sick in front of him.

"Wine, *señora?*"

Caitlin raised her gaze to meet his then looked away and shook her head. "No. Thank you."

"A pity. It is a very good wine." He poured himself a glass, and then sat back in his chair, relaxed and self-assured.

"I hope you are hungry. I had my chef prepare grilled lamb with white rice and pine nuts." His syrupy smooth voice affected her like a chilling breeze. "I wanted to prepare you something much more extravagant, but understand you have a delicate stomach."

Caitlin's breath caught in her throat, but she suppressed any outward acknowledgement of his words. The way he looked at her with a combination of malice and pity made her glad she had a chair beneath her. *Does he know? Did Maria tell him?*

Her gut lurched at the thought, but she tried to concentrate instead on the food. She didn't really have an appetite, but knew she should try to get some nourishment while she could. She reminded herself that she was in the company of a man who was as ruthless as he was handsome. It would do her no good to make him angry, yet she had no intention of pretending to respect or admire him.

"Eat a little." His voice was soft, yet sent another shiver down her spine. "You will feel better."

Caitlin accepted the food offered and ate slowly, reluctantly, and in silence. The fare was good, but impossible to swallow. How could she eat with his probing gaze upon her? He reminded her of a cat, calmly watching its prey before going in for the kill.

After a few minutes, she put her fork down and sat back.

Beneath his steady scrutiny she could not eat another bite. The candles, the expensive gold-rimmed china, the extravagant art on the walls were all a contradiction. She was dining in an elegant setting with a monster from hell.

"Is that all for you, *señora?* Surely you are not done eating."

"Yes, I am finished." She started to push away from the table. "I would like to go back to my prison…" She swallowed hard, lifted her head, and boldly met his gaze. "I mean, my room."

She saw the flash of emotion in his eyes again, but he successfully extinguished it before motioning for the waiters in the room to leave. "I would not think of letting you go without a little after-dinner conversation," he said smoothly. "Are you sure you would not like some wine? Eh?"

Caitlin did not bother to respond. She simply locked her gaze on a statue of an angel on the far side of the room, and prayed for the strength to get through this ordeal.

"As you wish." Carlos's voice was tinged with a mixture of anger and irritation. He poured himself another glass, and then began to pace beside the long table.

Caitlin tried to ignore the sound of his agitated footsteps as they struck the marble floor. She sat silently with her hands folded in her lap, staring straight ahead, trying to prepare herself for whatever was to come. He had already killed Blake. There would be no reason to keep her alive.

As if reading her mind, he spoke. "*Señora.* Do you know how close I came to telling Pedro to kill you? This is an aggravation I do not really need."

"I wish you would have."

She heard Carlos stop behind her, felt him stare at her, before he started laughing. Even though he was behind her, she felt his presence—and despite his laughter, he radiated nothing but violence and rage. When his fingers touched her hair, she jumped as if struck by a lightning bolt.

"But then I would never have gotten to see the spirit you possess," he said softly.

Caitlin bit her lip to keep from screaming.

"I have seen your hair in pictures," he said, continuing to run his fingers through her hair as if feeling its texture and softness. "We will let it grow again."

Caitlin jerked her head away, out if his reach. "Pictures of me?"

"Of course. Dozens, *señora*. I have studied your husband's family for a long time. The file is large."

Caitlin tried to control her voice. "I thought you wanted to kill me."

"Yes, but my plans have since changed."

"Why?" She turned and looked at him for the first time, curiosity getting the best of her.

"I wanted your husband to suffer."

Caitlin closed her eyes. "But he is dead."

"Yes, we will let it grow again." He continued the conversation about her hair as if the previous one had not taken place.

"When are you going to let me go?" She tried to change the subject, wanted to get him to stop talking like that.

"I do not believe I wish to let you go." Carlos pulled out the chair beside her and sat down. "As I said, plans change."

When Caitlin met his gaze, she watched something disturbing creep in, replacing the callous, angry look. It made the hair stand up on the back of her neck. A slow, purposeful smile began to spread across Carlos's face as he seemed to sense her fear. But the smile held no humor or warmth—only scorn and evil intentions.

He leaned in close. "I wish to make you an offer, *señora*."

"There is nothing in this world you can offer me that I want." She turned her head away from him. "You've taken *that* away from me."

"But in return, I can give you this." He waved his hand in the air. "Think of it, my dear. Lavish trips. Extravagant clothes. Luxury such as you can only imagine. Every indulgence you have ever dreamed about."

His face shined with an excited light, as if he thought she could not resist such an offering.

"I would rather *die*." Caitlin stood and pushed in her chair emphatically. "Thank you for dinner. I would like to return to my room."

When she looked at his face, she wondered how she had ever thought him handsome before. A cold and calculating expression darkened his features now, making him appear threatening and dangerous.

"Your husband's children would be orphans. You would be so unkind?"

The statement sucked the breath out of her, but she pretended to be unaffected. "He has provided for them. They will not be alone."

"I see." Carlos began to pace, the sound of his shoes

again drilling into Caitlin's strong reserve.

"And you would be so careless with the life you carry?"

The statement was so unexpected that Caitlin was unable to suppress her reaction. One hand instinctively moved to her stomach in a defensive position as the other went to the back of the chair to hold her up.

"How did you know?" Her voice wavered and her knees began to shake, but she squared her shoulders and lifted her chin to hide her emotions.

"I didn't." Carlos laughed, seeming to enjoy her struggle to regain her composure. "But I see the maternal instinct in you is strong."

"Perhaps that is what makes me wish to leave this place as soon as possible." Caitlin was able to keep her voice from shaking. Anger was beginning to replace the fear. Anger and revulsion.

"No. No. I feel obliged to extend my hospitality to you. It may seem strange to you now, but I think you will be happy here." He stood and walked behind her again, out of her sight.

Caitlin was glad he could not see her face. She found him so repulsive, she could barely keep herself from gagging. She began to sweat and to shiver simultaneously and had to concentrate on not passing out. She felt a raw despair settle upon her, dragging her down as she thought about a future here. Her eyes roamed the room and saw everything anyone could ever need—and nothing she would ever want.

He leaned down and whispered in her ear. "The ladies say I am quite talented. I do not believe you will be disappointed."

Caitlin jerked away, closing her eyes and biting her lip to keep from whimpering. "Do not touch me."

Carlos put his head back and laughed. "I like women who put up a fight." But then the laughter and all hint of humor left his voice. "But I must tell you, I tire of it quickly."

Caitlin did not know what he meant and did not ask for clarification.

"Perhaps Pedro told you that I have access to tools." He paused as if waiting for a reaction. "Tools that will turn a lion into a sheep."

Caitlin's shaking legs would no longer support her so she pulled out the chair and sat down.

"Yes, my dear. Even the most rebellious women succumb." He bent down and rubbed his thumb over her cheek. "In fact they *beg*."

"I can assure you," Caitlin said in a loud, distinct voice, "I will die before I beg for anything from you."

"When I am done with you, you will do as I say." He smiled. "Heroin has a way."

A shiver of revulsion ran through her, followed by a trembling she could not hide.

Carlos began to laugh. "I have put you in an awkward situation, I believe. No?"

She did not look at him. She couldn't.

"If you do not wish to become an addict—dependent and helpless and begging for your next fix—you have only to come to me willingly."

When she did not answer, he leaned down and whispered in her ear. "Do you understand me?"

Caitlin clenched her teeth to keep them from chattering. She did not want him to know how deeply he affected her.

"I must warn you, I'm an insatiable lover." He crossed his arms. "But by your silence, I believe I have my answer. No? You will stay with me."

Caitlin stared straight ahead, saying nothing. Not moving. A heavy blanket of despair had fallen upon her shoulders, and she was finding it difficult to breathe.

"Of course, I will be a gentleman and give you a few days to get acclimated to your new home." He put his hand across the left side of his chest and patted it twice. "See? I possess a soft heart."

Caitlin bit her quivering lip. "And when you tire of me?"

"My dear. It will be your job to make sure I do not tire of you." His voice was soft. "I have a feeling we will have a long time together."

Caitlin lowered her gaze to the table and focused her attention on a knife. Somehow, some way, she would slit his throat. Or she would slit her own. But his prophecy would not come to pass.

Chapter 28

Colt and Blake had both been working the phones. It would soon be time to launch the assault, and they needed to compare notes.

"What did you find?"

Colt threw a map on the hood of the truck and turned to Blake. "Bad news and more bad news."

"Bad news first." Blake didn't hesitate.

"Drone sensors show at least a hundred men." Colt leaned over the map and tried to get his bearings compared to what he'd seen on the drone footage. "There's a barracks over here. Big question is, how many more are hidden in tunnels or underground?"

"Okay. What's the other bad news?"

"The bad news is, I'm not sure the President will authorize me to lead a raid into a foreign country."

"That's okay," Blake said, shrugging his shoulders, "since I'll be leading it."

Colt's head tilted to the side as he stared into Blake's eyes. "You know I'm on your side, but I'm a little uncomfortable with the possibility of starting an international crisis over this."

"I could give a shit about an international crisis with a country who condones selling drugs and murdering innocent women and children." Blake's voice drew the attention of some of the other officers that remained on the scene.

Colt's phone buzzed just then, and he started to walk away to answer it.

"What's up with that ringtone?" Blake was suddenly standing right beside him. "You change it?"

Colt tried to wave him off, but he knew Blake was too astute to fall for a story. This ringtone was specifically for Podge on a special phone when he had urgent information. Colt didn't know if it was good news or bad, but he knew Podge wouldn't have used the phone unless absolutely necessary.

Colt looked skyward before pushing the button. *Not another obstacle. Please, not another one.*

"Go ahead." He held up his hand for quiet and turned his back so Blake couldn't read the emotions on his face.

"Good news and bad news," Podge said.

"Bad news first."

"No. I'll start with the good news. "That fence you're looking at is not the actual boundary line. It was just moved two weeks ago."

"You shitting me?" He turned around to stare at the fence.

"What's going on?" Blake stood in front of him now.

Colt lowered the phone a minute. "That's not the international boundary line. The fence was moved." He watched Blake let out his breath and lean against the truck in relief.

"You're positive?" Colt put the phone back up to his ear.

"Yeah. Carlos owns two thousand acres and moved that fence about two weeks ago according to satellite images we found. We double-checked the coordinates with the drones, and sure enough, it's within the U.S. border."

Colt joined Blake and leaned casually against the truck as he talked on the phone, as relaxed now as if he were discussing a football game on a Sunday afternoon. All that was missing was a beer in his hand. "So we're back to Plan A. We'll get some backup, maybe even a helicopter now. I was reluctant to tell the President because of the international ramifications, but he'll definitely be on board now."

"Not exactly," Podge said. "I didn't tell you the bad news yet."

Colt's heart dropped at the tone of Podge's voice, and he remembered that the call had been urgent.

"Go ahead."

"The President is no longer *requesting* your services."

Before he had time to question the statement, Podge finished his thought. "He's *ordering* you to another location."

"What are you talking about?"

"The feds have uncovered some intel that indicates Carlos has hooked up with ISIS."

"What in the hell are you talking about?"

"It's a long story, but it's credible. I'll let the alphabet agencies give you the details. But the kidnapping is just a diversion to much bigger things. Carlos knew Blake had some clout, and that he would throw all of the resources available at getting Cait back."

Colt pushed himself off the truck, walked around to the back, and lowered the tailgate before sitting down. "I'm putting you on speaker."

He laid the phone down and motioned for Blake to join

him. "Okay, so what's the plan?"

"You can expect a call from POTUS in about an hou
but I can tell you he wants you to jump off this and on to the
other task force."

"What task force is that?" Blake asked, thoroughly confused.

"They think Carlos has hooked up with ISIS." Colt filled
him in quickly. "This is a diversion to keep assets—or at least
our attention—from something bigger."

"Something bigger?" Blake sat down on the tailgate, letting out his breath as he did. "Like what?"

"Like what?" Colt repeated, his voice showing his concern.

"I'm sure you guys have both heard the reports that ISIS
stole radioactive material from an Iraqi university a few years
ago. Apparently, there've been some social media postings and
radio traffic out of Syria that say they've gotten their hands on
uranium from another university."

Both men exhaled loudly. "Do they have the capability to
do anything with it?"

"Iraq's United National Ambassador thinks so," Podge
said. "He's warning that these materials can be used in manu-
facturing weapons of mass destruction."

"Even though the amount they have is limited and isn't
weaponized?"

"Yeah. ISIS doesn't have known missile delivery capability, but they probably have the ability to create a dirty bomb.
It would be primitive, but would still involve an explosive that
would disseminate radioactive material."

ould ensue."

effective for scaring people, more so than

e terrorists are banking on the fear factor of

s what we're looking at here. In a place like DC, it would effectively shut the entire region down for weeks at least, if not months."

"Whoa. How did we make the leap from them *possessing* these materials to them being in the United States?"

"That's where Carlos comes in." There was a long pause. "I should probably let POTUS brief you."

"No. Go ahead. Give me the basics so I'm up to speed."

"Long story short, the Mexican Army and federal law enforcement ran across some documents in Arabic and Urdo, as well as the layout of Fort Bliss a while back."

"Where?"

"About fifteen miles south of you in Mexico."

Colt glanced over at the intense look on Blake's face. "Go on."

"Well, all along, Homeland Security has been downplaying the threat, saying the border is secure, but the President is taking the threat seriously now."

"Now? Why now?"

Podge exhaled. "It appears the Coyotes who work for Carlos in human smuggling are guiding the ISIS terrorists through the desert. They know that area is understaffed as far as border patrol goes, and it's already a safe haven for Carlos's large-scale drug smuggling."

"If we know where they're coming in, why don't we stop it?"

"They're working on it. Some of this information is coming from a Syrian national they caught entering the country illegally, and he says it's too late. They're already here."

"With the dirty bomb materials?"

"Apparently," Podge said. "The CIA is working on that side of it. But Carlos has an airstrip."

"Do they know their intentions?"

"Not yet, but they nailed a Mexican national attempting to join ISIS. No word on whether or not he's talking—or if he knows anything."

"Da-a-mn." Colt looked at Blake and then put his head in his hands, rubbing his temples. Why did everything have to be so complicated? Why did he have to choose between saving his best friend's wife and possibly saving his country?

"What's the urgency?" He tried to stall. "Do they have definite intel on a timeline?"

"Not that I'm aware of. But the President is gathering a task force, and he wants you to lead it. You need to get your butt back to the east coast. There's a hostage rescue unit from Homeland Security that's been sent to take your place there."

Colt shook his head. "We're close here. Tell the President to give me a few hours. I have business to take care of."

"This isn't a *suggestion*, Colt. It's an order. The President wants you in DC."

"I can hardly hear you," Colt said loudly, picking up the phone, holding it at arm's length. "I think we're losing our signal." He pushed the button to end the call.

"Don't." Blake grabbed his arm when he realized what Colt was doing, but it was too late. "Call him back. I can handle things here. You go."

"No. Ancient Chinese proverb say... 'If you chase two rabbits, both will escape.'" Colt used a bad Chinese accent as he said the words.

"What the f—?"

"Zip it." Colt held up his hand for silence. "I've already got a plan in my head to get Caitlin. We'll get this done, and then I'll go. You know how they are in that town. Not making a decision and then all of a sudden it's a crisis."

Colt walked to the driver's side of the truck and opened the door. "I'll make some calls from here to get things rolling. A few hours without me onsite isn't going to make a difference."

"Colt. It's POTUS. It's national security. I think you better go."

"It's Cait. I'm staying. Shut the fuck up." Colt nonchalantly pulled out a map and unfolded it as he walked to the hood of the truck and laid it out. "According to the drone footage and the intel I got from local police, the outer perimeter of sentinels looks to be about here. They seem to be pretty stationary, so you shouldn't have much trouble getting in between them."

Colt glanced up at Blake. "You do want to go in first, right?"

Blake nodded and leaned back over the map. There was no need for words.

"I'll be right behind you; plus, we got about a dozen guys for backup. I can round up some more manpower locally, but it's still going to be a little hairy. We need to get in and get out."

"Is one of you guys Nicholas Colton?"

Both men turned around at exactly the same time. Both sets of eyes traveled to the round-faced brunette woman who'd spoken, and then to the Homeland Security insignia on her jacket.

"Who's asking?" Colt crossed his arms and leaned against the truck, but threw a sideways glance at Blake. He could see he was thinking the same thing: *BOHIC. Bend Over Here It Comes.*

"I am." Her eyes narrowed at his elusive remark. "Agent Trish Peterson with CTTU. You Colton?"

Colt's heart sank. The Counter Terrorism Tactical Unit, a newly created division of Homeland Security was a situational disaster by anyone's standards. He heard Blake whisper under his breath, "Thanks, Mr. President."

Colt shot Blake a sideways glance that said let-me-handle-this, and then answered the woman. "Maybe. Why you want to know?"

"We've been directed to take over here, and I'm assigning you to provide perimeter security and backup. I need to make sure we're on the same page."

Colt put his hand on Blake's shoulder to keep him from jumping in on the conversation and then took a step closer to the woman. "We're apparently *not* on the same page. I'm with Phantom Force Tactical, and we're taking the lead."

"Permission denied."

Colt's eyes narrowed, and then he laughed. "You misunderstood. I wasn't asking for *permission.*"

"Good. Then, like I said, you'll be providing backup."

Colt stuck his hands in his pockets so she wouldn't see

the fists he was making as he sized her up—all five feet five inches and one hundred eighty or so pounds. He could see in an instant that this was a woman who'd been handed a job she wasn't qualified for by someone who wasn't qualified to be handing out jobs. She had delusions of grandeur and was in over her head—a fact that everyone except she understood.

"You can see where being backup has gotten us." Colt nodded toward the demolished house. He leaned back against the truck in a relaxed manner despite the anger and frustration surging through his veins.

She ignored him. "Our hostage rescue team is the first in. We're trained to do this. And we've wanted to take down Carlos for a long time."

"How many hostage rescues have you done?"

"That's not the point," she snapped.

"What *is* the point?"

"The point is, I'm in charge. Whether or not you follow my orders and take part is entirely up to you."

"Correction." Colt didn't blink, and he didn't look away. "The point isn't whether or not we go—but how and when."

Her eyes turned to mere slits, but her voice sounded calm. She knew her position gave her the authority to order him to leave the premises if she so desired. "We're debriefing in thirty minutes. If you want to be in on this, be there."

Colt took pride in his self-control, but for a brief moment, he thought perhaps he'd lose it. This was an agency that needed to prove their worth. Their objective was to bag Carlos and get the hostage out one way or the other—which was the same thing as saying: dead or alive.

"You do understand we're dealing with DMFPs, right?" His voice was calm, as if he'd just asked her about the weather.

"I beg your pardon?"

"Dangerous Mother Fucking People!" Blake had controlled himself through the exchange and now stepped forward, practically shouting the words.

Colt grabbed him by the arm to quiet him and then turned back to the agent. He spoke in the most controlled tone he could muster. "The problem here, ma'am, is that lives are at stake—"

She cut him off with an angry wave of her hand. "I understand what's at stake. That's why we're going to *negotiate*." Her eyes darted from one man to the other, daring them to defy her. "I don't need any trigger-happy cowboy yahoos storming the gates while we're trying to talk."

Colt looked at Blake and winked so he would know to play along. The situation was now so out of control it was almost funny—or would be, if the stakes weren't so high. In any event, it was obvious nothing they said was going to get her to back down, reconsider, or take advice from those who had done this hundreds of times before. "Bro, did she just call us trigger-happy cowboy yahoos?"

Blake nodded. "Never been called *that* before."

"Me either." Colt shook his head. "I don't think I even know what that means."

"I'll tell you what it means…" The calm tones of the men seemed to anger her. "I can't have members of the media put in harm's way because a couple of loose cannons can't follow orders."

"Wait. What do you mean, *media?*" His calm, controlled façade vanished, replaced by cold, hard fury.

She must have noticed the change. Colt watched varying degrees of fear, contempt, suspicion, and agitation play upon her face before she responded. Then she nodded toward a satellite truck chugging up the road. "CNN. They are going to stay strictly where I tell them, but they have exclusive rights to the video."

"So this is a publicity stunt for you?" He gave her a glance of utter disbelief.

"Don't worry." She patted his arm. "Even if you don't take part, I'll make sure your name gets in the press release— as long as you don't cause any trouble."

Self-control be damned. The fact that the person standing in front of him was a woman was the only thing that kept Colt from laying her out flat—and he was quickly reaching the point where even that wasn't going to matter.

"Why don't you show CNN the tunnel?" Colt nodded toward the demolished house. "Maybe they can beat us to Carlos." The words were said sarcastically, but she had apparently already considered the possibility.

"The tunnel is demolished on this end. At least the first fifty feet. It either collapsed during the house explosion or was blown on purpose."

That's what I figured. "What do you need us to do?" Colt pretended to sound agreeable, but he wasn't sure he was successful.

"We're going in at zero four hundred hours. We probably won't need you guys, but I want you to be ready to help out if we run into the unexpected."

"Great plan." Colt looked at Blake and nodded. "What time you moving into position?"

He glanced over at Blake to make sure he knew Colt was just playing along. To an outsider, Blake appeared calm and in control, but Colt could tell he was close to detonating. His stance revealed a great reserve of suppressed power that had reached its limit—like a pressure cooker ready to blow.

She looked at her watch. "We'll start getting into position at zero three hundred."

"We'll be good to go..."

She stared at Colt a moment as if assessing his sincerity and then turned.

"At zero one hundred." Colt finished his sentence under his breath once she had walked way.

Chapter 29

"We're sure as hell not providing backup." Blake didn't talk quietly and barely waited for her to get out of hearing range.

"No. We just have to move our schedule up. We shove off in an hour. We'll be in and on our way by the time they're getting into position."

"The sooner the better," Blake muttered, raking his hand through his disheveled hair. "That PITA will find a way to screw this up if we don't move quickly."

Colt let the slang word for Pain In The Ass slip by without comment. "I'd call the President and tell him to call them off, but I'm not exactly in his good graces right now."

"Yeah, you dug yourself a hole there."

"But it's all working out for the better. We'll move early because of the feds. Then we'll get this taken care of, and I'll get to DC before the President even knows I've delayed him."

"Yeah. Funny how great things are working out." Blake's voice had a hint of sarcasm in it. "I thought you'd get some downtime though for a quick combat nap."

Colt had no comment. He knew people didn't understand the long hours he could work with no diminishment in judgment or equilibrium, but it was just part of his makeup. He couldn't sleep in the middle of an important mission like this.

He'd catch up when it was over.

Blake turned and began studying the map again, while Colt's gaze remained on the activity growing around the woman, as other troops under her direction continued to arrive. "This feminist shit is going to get someone killed."

"You got that right." Blake looked up and followed Colt's gaze. "We both know some women can handle the job, but you can't give a high-level position to someone just to fill a quota. It's a recipe for disaster."

Colt rubbed his fingers over his throbbing temples. He needed to stop thinking about that and concentrate on the problem at hand. He needed to make decisions about a mission he was unsure of, against an enemy's size he was uncertain of, on a battlefield he'd never stepped foot on.

But he had experience behind him. And experience had taught them that the advantage was gained by those who projected the most violence. He glanced at Blake. *No one is going to have any illusions about who that is.*

"Okay. Where were we?" Colt instantly fell back into place. This was his world. He belonged here. He leaned over the map on the hood of the truck again and noticed the burned paint and scratches. "Glad we weren't in that UPS of yours when that house blew."

Blake looked over the hood at him. "UPS?"

"Unprotected piece of shit."

"Yeah, good thing you fortified this thing, isn't it? Some of those police cars didn't hold up too well."

"Nice call, boss." Colt was glad Blake didn't bring up how he had resisted Blake's suggestion to get bullet proof glass and extra steel plating on the truck. It had made it a big, heavy gas guzzler—but now it seemed worth every extra penny he'd spent on fuel.

Colt returned to business and pointed at the map. "So while we're breaching the house, I'll have teams deployed here, and here—in case they are alerted. If we have to, we'll knock them off as quickly and quietly as we can."

"But they'll be warned at some point."

Colt looked up. "We're going to give you as much time as we can."

"Getting in isn't going to be a problem." Blake shrugged. "Getting out could get…complicated."

"Roger that." There was no need for further comment. In their line of work, conditions were rarely perfect, yet they accepted the danger and inevitable chaos that would ensue—especially in this case.

"We got one thing going for us. According to Podge and the drone footage, they seldom deviate from their regular patrols. Podge is working on a map right now, overlaying the times the ATV and foot patrols hit certain points of the property.

"What are the rules of engagement?" Blake asked the question in a voice that suggested he didn't care one way or the other.

"Terminate anyone who's a threat."

"Good deal." Blake nodded, accepting that answer. "And just to be clear, even if I make contact early, Charlie Mike."

"Got it. Continue Mission." Colt knew Blake would rather go down fighting if there was no chance of rescue than make it out alive. He walked to the other side of the truck, pulled down his zipper, and relieved himself. "But don't get any ideas about being a cowboy in there," he said when he was done. "Right?"

"I'm not planning to send Carlos to prison if that's what you're asking." Blake opened the door and shot Colt a smile that carried no humor in it as he settled onto the seat. "Matter of fact, I'm planning on sending him to Hell."

Colt knew this was serious. Blake wasn't the kind of man to make a threat. Only a commitment.

"Your objective and your orders are to bring out Caitlin." Colt jumped into the truck and stuck his finger in Blake's face. "That's it. Got it?"

Blake was busy looking for updates on his phone but gave an if-you-say-so shrug without bothering to look up. "Yep, I got it."

"Do justice. Show mercy. That's what you always tell us. Remember?" Colt made one last attempt to talk some sense into his friend.

"I remember." Blake put down his phone and pulled out his Glock. "I'm not saying I'm going to enjoy killing him." He looked up at Colt with chilling blue eyes that said *I will hurt someone*. "I'm saying I accept the necessity."

Colt saw the expression and knew that the military training so deeply ingrained in Blake had lifted to the surface again. He was a soldier, and it sparked, burned, and blazed from every fiber of his being. Colt closed his eyes a moment and then stared into the distance at the house they would be assaulting.

May God have mercy on their souls, because Blake won't.

Chapter 30

Colt looked up to see about a dozen heavily armed men walking up the road toward his truck.

"Maybe these are my guys," he said to no one in particular. He knew Podge had been busy trying to round up as many Phantom Force guys as he could.

"Yo, Colt!" A tall, broad-shouldered young man with an M-4 hanging casually across his chest strode toward him with his hand extended.

"No way." Colt stepped forward to shake his hand, and ended up throwing his arm around his shoulders as well in a rare display of affection. "If it isn't Weston Armstrong. You are a sight for sore eyes, brother."

"Hey, Wes." Blake strode over and pumped his hand a few times. "Who in the hell do we owe for dragging your ass into this? I thought you were deployed."

"Podge, of course." The man laughed, his deep gray eyes dancing with amusement. "Landed about two hours ago. Podge sent transportation and here I am." He turned around and waved his hand. "Along with a few of my closest friends."

He took a step closer and lowered his voice. "Podge said you'd cover my ass if there were any ramifications."

"You got it. A full freaking pardon if it comes to that. You just made our day a whole lot brighter." Colt took a deep breath of relief. Wes was still active duty and about ten years his junior, but if there was anyone besides Blake he wanted in a fight, it was him. Colt had served a few years with Wes back when he was a NFG on the team. He was a natural soldier back then and had earned a reputation as one hell of a warrior in the years following.

"Sorry about Caitlin." Wes turned to Blake. "We'll get her back."

Blake nodded. "Thanks, brother. Thanks for being here."

"Okay." Colt motioned everyone forward. "Gather 'round. I'll show you the lay of the land."

"I actually have someone with me who knows the house on the inside if you're interested."

"Holy shit, yeah." Colt felt a sense of relief surge through him. Were things finally going to start going right?

"Where's Hogan?" Wes turned around and scanned the group of men.

"Lagging behind," one of the men said good-naturedly as the others stepped aside, forming a pathway for a figure walking with head bent intently over a tablet computer.

"Gentlemen, this is Tori Hogan. She was with the DEA. I thought she might be an asset here."

Colt studied the figure who had still not looked up from the computer. *She? Great. Another one. Just great.* His heart plummeted.

But when she did look up, he had to put his hand on the side of the truck to steady himself. The deep brown, oval-shaped eyes that rested on him briefly matched those he saw every night when he closed his own eyes. He gazed down at the Glock holstered on her thigh, and for just a moment, his mind went back.

"One minute to target."

The thwap, thwap, thwap of the helicopter blades slicing through the air made conversation impossible. Colt offered Griff a nod of his head and a thumbs up sign as she sat on the opposite side of the chopper. She would be translating and helping communicate with the hostages, all of whom were foreigners. Once things got started, he probably wouldn't see her again until the exfil.

She returned his gesture by shooting him a one-finger salute with both hands. He couldn't see her expression from beneath the hijab she wore, but he knew she was smiling.

His gaze slid down to her hands that were now expertly cradling her rifle, then focused again on her face. She appeared calm. Fearless. The sexiest thing he'd ever seen. Maybe he'd tell her that when they got back to the FOB.

Her eyes remained locked on his with a questioning look, as if she were trying to decipher what he was thinking.

She must have figured it out because when the order to move was given, she winked.

Colt jerked back to the present when Blake shook him by the shoulder. "Yo, brother, they're talking to you."

"Here you go." Tori Hogan stood right in front of him now, holding out her tablet. She was all business.

"We raided that property about five years ago." She continued to thumb through some photos. "They must have gotten tipped off because it was clean. Here's what I have."

She put the tablet down on the tailgate while Colt and Blake leaned in on each side of her.

"So, here's the gate on this side, the north."

Both men nodded.

"When they're expecting a delivery, they have at least

two men posted checking ID, but for the most part, it's just locked. Carlos does most of his personal travel by helicopter or plane."

"Good to know, but we're not planning to use the gate."

"I didn't think so," she said, matter-of-factly, "but if you need an emergency egress for ambulatory reasons, you're going to need explosives. It's not just for show. It's solid."

"We've got what we need for the job if it comes to that." Colt punched some notes into his phone that he'd send to Podge. It was always good to be prepared for the worst-case scenario. This woman knew her stuff.

As for Tori Hogan, she didn't look impressed that he was prepared for such an eventuality, or even particularly surprised. This was apparently routine for her.

"You can see the wall goes all the way around. It's eight feet high and two feet wide. From here,"—she pointed to the gate—"to here"—she pointed to the first step of the porch—"is thirty yards."

Colt looked up at Blake. "Got that?"

Blake nodded. Twelve strides once he got over the wall.

"Okay, then it's up four steps, and fifteen feet to the front door. The door opens *out*."

Both men looked at each other. "You sure?"

"I'm sure."

"Roger that." Colt's gaze met Blake's, both of them remembering an op in which they had used explosives thinking the door was locked. Instead, it had just opened the other way.

"Now to the layout of the inside." Hogan slid her finger across the screen. "I only have this one photo, and it's not very clear, but you can get the idea."

The men leaned in close.

"It's your typical Spanish layout. Large foyer. Steps are to your right. There are twelve. Once upstairs, the rooms run across the balcony that overlooks the interior of the house."

"And balconies on the exterior, as well?"

She nodded. "Yes. Each room has a balcony facing the pool."

"What about tunnels?"

Hogan looked up at Colt with a grave expression. "We know they're there, but we didn't find any. They may start somewhere else on the property. That was the thinking back then anyway."

"Or they weren't dug yet," Blake said.

"Could be. He had only been at that location for about two years before that raid."

Colt and Blake looked at each other with eager expressions. The information she'd provided was invaluable. With the distances mapped out, Blake could get to the second floor of the house with his eyes closed if he had to. His brain could be concentrating on other things because it wouldn't have to be learning the layout as he went.

Colt looked at his watch. "I asked Podge for some guys to secure the perimeter and pull security once we're in. Basically, keep any reinforcements out."

"I guess that's us," Wes said.

"But I'm thinking now I could use you to split this team, create a diversion with one half, infiltrate behind us with the other." He looked at Wes. "You good with that?"

"I'm good." He turned around. "You guys good?"

There was a general nodding of heads as they gathered closer and listened to Colt's plan. When everyone was comfortable with what they would be doing, Colt stepped back. "We've got some feds here breathing down our necks, so play it cool and keep it quiet," he said. "We're moving out in forty-five."

The group moved away to gather their equipment and prepare for their role in the operation, while Colt turned and started walking toward the front of the truck.

"You two have a history?"

"What?" Colt glanced back at Blake with a furrowed brow but kept walking.

"You sleep with that woman before?"

"What in the hell are you talking about?"

"That Hogan woman. The DEA agent. Did you sleep with her?"

"I repeat. What in the *hell* are you talking about?" Colt pulled a bottle of water from a small cooler and took a long swallow, but his eyes never left Blake's.

"I don't know. Something about the look that flashed across your face. Just for an instant... And damn if it didn't flash across her face, too."

"You're full of—" Colt spit water and almost choked when he started talking before he'd swallowed. "Shit."

"And another thing," Blake said, ignoring Colt's response. "You were smiling."

Colt shot him a perturbed look. "Pretty sure I smile all the time."

"No. No. It wasn't the polite-Colt smile. We're talking the real thing."

"Maybe you read the I-want-you look on *her* face but not on mine. I can't help that I'm a chick magnet." He rested both arms on the side of his truck and stared at nothing as he thought about the scene that had played out before his eyes—not the woman who had caused the memory. "She winked at me."

"That woman?" Blake clapped his hands together. "I knew it."

"No." Colt glanced over his shoulder at Blake with a look of disgust. "Griff. On the helo on that last op. It was like she was telling me everything was okay. Maybe it's an omen."

"She saved a lot of lives." Blake's tone grew low. "She made the choice to do that."

Something about those words caused pain to spread like a poison through Colt's veins. It was a pain both ancient and fresh. "That doesn't make it any easier."

"I know, brother. I'm sorry about that." Blake gave Colt's shoulder a squeeze. "And I'm sorry about misreading that look you gave Hogan."

Colt took another slug of water and twisted the cap back on the bottle. "No problem."

"Yeah. Glad we got that straight. It was definitely an I-*want*-to-sleep-with-her look, not an oh-shit-I-slept-with-her look."

"Go to hell, Blake." When Colt glanced over his shoulder at his friend, he saw the makings of a sly smile—the first he'd seen in days. He understood why. Now that they had a plan and a target, Blake had some control over the situation. He was confident and secure in his abilities; all he needed was the opportunity. Facing bullets was nothing compared to the wait. Still, Colt was somewhat amazed at the man's stoic calm.

"Shit's going to hit the fan soon. You sure you're ready?"

"I'm more than ready." Blake's tone grew serious, and his eyes took on a faraway look as he gazed at the house in the distance, his expression toggling between confidence and breathless anticipation

"Let's go get this thing done."

Chapter 31

Colt put his truck in gear and drove down the long, dusty lane toward the house, noticing how a line of small trees along the road glowed like golden sentries in the moonlight.

His mission was to gain intelligence on where exactly Caitlin was being held so they didn't have to waste time searching the grounds. Under different circumstances, the sight of the soft, white moonlight blanketing the wide expanse of desert would have conveyed a sense of peace—if not security. But that's the last thing he was thinking about tonight. No, tonight he was thinking about the enemy—and how to kill them.

The sound of the wheels rolling across the sandy dirt road made Colt feel right at home. His blood surged with anticipation, and his senses were pegged on high alert—but he felt no fear. In fact, the thrill and excitement were so strong and satisfying, he felt guilty. It had taken him twenty years to learn that not everyone was born with this silent, secret hunger for pandemonium. Some people thought it strange, but he would rather die on his feet than live a life where he could overdose on stability and tranquility.

It wasn't long before a man stepped out of the darkness into the brightness of his headlights, pointing a gun at him. Slamming on the brakes, Colt raised his hands, making sure the bottle of Tequila he held was clearly visible. The guard walked over to the window and banged on it with his gun.

"What are you doing here?" he bellowed in Spanish, waving his gun back and forth. "Turn around."

Colt lowered his window. "Whoa, *hombre*. Calm down."

The man looked at him with anger and suspicion, but that didn't bother Colt. He had a way of getting people to tell him what he wanted—usually without much trouble, and almost never with any significant resistance.

"Do you sh-peak English?" Colt slurred his words and leaned closer, even though the smell almost made him wince.

The man moved in closer as well and stuck the barrel of his gun through the window. "No Engleesh!"

Colt grabbed the gun and gave it a jerk, knocking the man off balance and pulling him closer to the window. Then he drew back his fist and sucker punched the guy in the face. Hard. "Here's a quick lesson. In English, that means I don't like your attitude."

As the man instinctively went for the trigger, Colt grabbed his hand and bent it backward until it snapped, causing the Mexican to shift all of his attention to the pain in his extremity. It was a piece of cake then for Colt to pull the man's body half in and half out of the window, and hit the button for the window to go up, trapping the man's head and arms in the cab. "And this means, 'I need some information.'"

The man wailed, kicked, bucked, and struggled for a mo-

ment, then pleaded with bulging eyes when he saw no remorse.

In perfect Spanish, Colt interrogated him, and satisfied
with the answers, pulled out some zip ties. After disarming the
man and dislodging him from the window, Colt hog-tied him
and placed him along the side of the road. "Enjoy the rest,
hombre. You earned it."

"Fury One to Thunderbolt, I have a location for the PC."

"Go ahead, Fury One."

For the first time, Colt heard a twinge in Blake's voice
and regretted referring to his wife as PC, standard lingo for
Precious Cargo.

"Top of the stairs. Second room on the left."

"Roger that."

"The guards do a comms check every hour, so we have…"
Colt glanced at his watch. "Thirty-five minutes until they start
noticing they've got some guys missing."

"Ready to roll."

"I'll give you three minutes to get into place. Then the rest
of us move."

"Roger, Fury One. I'm moving. Over."

Colt took a deep breath and said a quick prayer. He was
confident and at ease, but it was moments like this, when he
was on the brink, that his memory would kick into overdrive.

Something in Griff's expression told Colt things weren't
quite right. As the hostages talked to her, she nodded that
she understood, her gaze searching the room until she found
what she was looking for.

Colt saw the man her gaze was locked on and walked toward him, too—just as a transmission came across the radio: "Be aware, we may have a combatant mixed in with the hostage population." Colt instinctively raised his weapon and hastened his stride. He was close enough now to see Griff's deep brown eyes turn from utter calm to alarm as the man reached for something under his garment. She shouted in Arabic, "Stop. Raise your hands." But he did not comply. Colt yelled for the hostages who stood frozen in front of him to move, but he knew he didn't have a clear shot or time to engage. Griff knew it, too. They were approaching from opposite sides of the room and were in each other's line of fire. Instead of risking the shot, she lunged, headfirst, and hit the man low in his stomach, driving him back, away from the others in the room.

Then the world exploded and everything went black.

Chapter 32

With the help of night vision goggles, Blake had no trouble passing through the outer perimeter of the compound, but he knew things would get dicey once he breached the outer fence—and he was right.

He stopped a moment and waited, knowing a patrol would be coming by in an ATV, and within minutes, he heard the sound of the engine approaching from the west. Lining the man up in his sights, he considered taking the shot but passed it up. The others might come looking for him. It would be better to let him make his rounds for now.

Anyway, Colt could handle him if it came to that. He did this type of thing for a living—it was just another day at work for him. And Blake knew there was nobody better. Colt was the poster child for an elite operator. Sometimes he wondered if he didn't have fire and gasoline pumping through his veins rather than blood.

When the vehicle rolled out of sight, Blake spoke into his radio.

"Ready to move."

"Wall is clear. You should have five minutes until the next patrol."

"Roger that."

There was no time to blink or think. Blake had to move.

He took off at a full run for the wall, jumped as high as he could, and clawed his way over the top. Dropping down the other side, he lay in the shadows, trying to catch his breath. Finally, he clicked on his mic. "I'm inside."

"Copy. Take a minute to catch your breath, old man."

"Fuck you, Colt," he whispered.

In reality, Blake was sucking air pretty good and was glad for the surge of adrenaline running through his veins. Otherwise, he knew he'd probably be down for the count. He hadn't been on an operation like this for years, and his body was letting him know it. But Caitlin was close—practically within reach. Nothing was going to stop him now.

Taking one last deep breath, Blake studied the house. Under the cover of darkness and within the shadowed depths of the elaborate landscaping, he could move faster than he'd done over the open terrain. Faster, but no less cautiously.

Although he was still about fifty yards away, he could make out a man sitting in a chair on the porch, holding an AK in his lap. He seemed to be dozing, but his finger was on the trigger.

"I have a visual on a tango at twelve o'clock."

Blake heard Colt's calm, methodical voice in his earpiece and knew he was somewhere right behind him.

"I see him."

Blake knew there would be no way to get by the guard. He took aim and pulled the trigger, the sound of his gun no louder than that of a staple gun. But just as the man slumped forward, he noticed movement and watched another guard approach from the side of the house; apparently having just relieved himself. The barrel of Blake's rifle swung over, and within a split second, that man was on the ground, too.

"Two tangos down." Blake took off running again and stopped only long enough to grab a radio from the dead man in the chair and push him back to an upright position so that it looked like he was just sleeping. If there were an unexpected radio check and these two didn't answer, he wanted to know about it.

"Making entry," Blake alerted Colt that he'd made it to the door. He knew that once the enemy fired the first shot, Phantom Force, with Colt leading the way, would strike swiftly, suddenly, and with no remorse. Colt's philosophy was simple. Blake had heard it repeated a thousand times: *There is no substitute for violence of action and volume of fire. Move forward and shoot. They will either choose to fight and die or live and run. Either way, move forward and fire.*

Lifting the large latch and giving it a pull, Blake assumed the door would not be locked considering all of the security outside—and it wasn't. But he wasn't anticipating the low growl of a large dog as soon as he entered. He swung his rifle around to the right and zeroed in with his laser on the Rottweiler's chest. Before it could bark, he pulled the trigger. Again, the gun made only a soft whoosh, and the dog dropped without making a sound. *Damn! A shitty way to start.* He had to take a few deep breaths to get his mind back in the game. Taking out Carlos was one thing. Killing a dog just protecting its home didn't sit well with him.

But in a clinical voice that belied the danger and the stakes, he simply said, "Moving to the second floor now."

Proceeding to the steps, he pointed his gun up and swiveled it back and forth, looking for targets. All was quiet. Treading as softly as possible, he studied the picture he saw through his night vision. The hall was eerily green and hazy, but he could see the ostentatious rugs and paintings, ornate moldings, and trim. He stopped in front of the second door on the left, leaned in close, and listened. Silence.

He shifted his gaze to the doorknob where a key was lodged. *Got the right room. No one locks a door from the outside.*

He slowed his heart by concentrating on his breathing as he unlocked the door. It clicked—loudly, he thought— but then his nerves were acutely attuned to the scene. A few adrenaline-soaked seconds later, he had pulled the door open and stepped inside, his weapon at the ready. As he started to scan to his right, a sudden movement to his left put him instantly on the defensive. He reached out and grabbed the arm that was trying to crack his skull with a vase and turned it violently.

The soft gasp of pain that followed nearly tore a hole in his heart. "Cait?"

The figure stopped moving as if frozen by an invisible wand. At the same time, the traffic in his earpiece picked up, and he could hear sporadic gunfire coming from outside. The guns were loud—definitely not the weapons of anyone on his team because they all used silencers.

"Contact by the front gate. Engaged."

The diversion had started early, but would provide cover for a little while.

Colt's clear, calm voice came over the earpiece. "Engage targets at will. If overrun, initiate the evacuation plan."

Blake ignored the chatter and turned toward the figure. "Cait. It's me."

Cait came to life now, but barely. She reached out and touched his arm like she thought she was touching a ghost.

"It's me," he said again.

He had planned to be all business and treat her like a normal hostage, but something in her look overwhelmed him and made him ache, so he drew her into his arms.

"You're not d-d-ead?"

He allowed himself to savor the feel of her in his arms for just a moment. The hardest thing he'd ever done in his life was pull away. "We have to hurry. Understand?" Her eyes were locked on his, calm and hopeful. She seemed to soak up his confidence.

As she nodded, he turned and took a few steps toward the balcony door to get a better sense of the battlefield outside. Muzzle flashes erupted from both the left and right, indicating pretty much everyone was actively engaged, but he could hear the surreal, calming cadence of water trickling from a fountain below them. The soothing sound, coupled with the chaotic bursts of fury from AKs, were a complete contradiction—something he often ran into on the battlefield.

Now that he had Cait within his grasp, his body kicked into auto-pilot, just like it had done on missions in his younger years. He was calm and he was focused. The commotion of gunfire outside was more a distraction than a real concern to him. It was not unexpected, and it wouldn't slow him down.

He'd just started to turn back around when he heard Cait let out a startled shriek. Whirling around completely, he saw a shadowy figure emerge from the doorway. Blake raised his gun, but in an instant, Carlos had Cait around the neck with one arm and a pistol to her head with the other. "I was not expecting you, *gringo*."

"Let her go, Carlos." Blake's sole focus was the man's finger on the trigger. "It's me you want."

"What I want is for you to see your wife die right before your eyes." Carlos emitted a sound like laughter, a cackle full of evil intent. "I could not have planned such a perfect ending if I had tried. Happy Anniversary...to all of us." He pressed the muzzle of the gun to her temple.

Blake's gaze shifted to Cait's face just as she closed her eyes. He knew she didn't do it from pain—or even fear. She did it to save him. She didn't want her eyes to haunt him when he watched her last moments on Earth...one year to the day when they had said their vows.

"Anything you want is yours, Carlos." He jerked his attention back to Carlos. "*Anything*. Just let her go."

In no battle had Blake's heart hammered as painfully as it did now. He felt helpless. He had no shot. The coward had placed Cait expertly between them, so there was no way Blake could fire without hitting her. He considered trying to tackle Carlos, to knock the gun from its aim, but he was at least three steps away. In the split second it would take Carlos to pull the trigger, Blake would never make it.

Concentrating on nothing but Carlos, Blake was vaguely aware that the sound of gunfire had changed from a spattering to a full-blown battle in the yard right below them. The voices in his earpiece were constant, but they were calm and methodical, like pool players calling their shots during a high-stakes backroom game.

"Put down your gun, *señor*."

Blake raised one hand to show he was complying and started to lower his weapon. "Okay. Just let her go. She has nothing to do with this."

"Nothing to do with this? She is your wife. Carrying your child."

Cait let out an involuntary gasp and then bit her lip to keep from repeating the mistake, which caused Carlos to laugh.

"Yes, I get two for the price of one." He lifted his hand slightly to better position the barrel resting against the side of her head. "Watch closely. Now you will know how it feels to lose someone you love."

Blake watched helplessly as the man's finger began to slowly apply pressure to the trigger.

Chapter 33

Blake never heard the shot. All he saw was the blood spurting onto Cait's lacy gown and drenching the back of her head.

The first bullet jerked Carlos's wrist and caused his fingers to fly open. His head lurched backward almost simultaneously as another bullet struck him there. It seemed like everything moved in slow motion until Carlos's pistol—and then his body—hit the floor, forcing Blake back to the present.

He lunged forward and pulled Cait into his arms before turning to see the figure coming through the balcony door.

"Everybody good here?" Colt sauntered into the room while casually slamming a fresh magazine into his gun. He reminded Blake of some great warrior robot, programmed for victory, calm, and immune to chaos. His voice was loud over the din of the battle going on outside, but his demeanor was unruffled. Unafraid. Composed. Commanding.

"Getting pretty hot out there." Colt walked toward the opposite door without stopping and motioned for them to follow. "Let's take the stairs."

Blake could feel the intensity of Colt's concentration and focus almost like a physical force. A normal man would have stopped and given Cait a hug or at least acknowledged that he had just saved her life. But Colt's job was not yet done. She was still in danger. His mind was already engaged in figuring out their next move—and the one after that.

Even though Blake had worked side-by-side with Colt for almost two decades, he was still a little in awe. The man didn't even sound out of breath, despite the fact he'd had to fight every inch of the way across the yard, and then somehow climb up to the second-story balcony fully kitted out. Colt possessed the added gift of being able to keep all emotion from his voice even when deep in the worst of it—or maybe he was living in a separate reality from what was going on around him. He'd just prevented a horrific tragedy, and was now calmly going about the necessity of extracting them all safely. Blake was doubly glad his friend had refused to go back to DC, choosing instead to see this thing through.

Blake could feel Cait shaking in his arms, but they had to move. He grabbed a blanket off the bed as they walked by and wiped the worst of the blood off as he maneuvered her toward the door. Try as he might, he couldn't resist glancing back at the body lying sprawled on the floor. It hadn't happened the way he'd planned it, but dead was dead.

He was brought back to the present when he heard Colt call out for a situation report over the radio. The teams outside reported they were still heavily engaged, but the backup team was working to secure the perimeter.

"PC in place for extraction." Colt gave his own sitrep into the mic. "Repeat, Precious Cargo ready for extraction. We'll be coming out the front door."

Blake placed Cait between them and guided her toward the door. "Follow Colt. Hang on to his shirt. Do what he says.

You're safe now."

There was no hesitation between the two men. No wasted effort. No questions or indecision. They moved together as one, communicating without words, and operating without fear.

Cait looked up at Blake with tears of relief gathering in her eyes and whispered, "I knew you would come."

Her voice, the mere sound of it, squeezed Blake's heart like a fist and caused his gut to knot. Despite his words of comfort, he knew they weren't out of danger yet. A lot could still go wrong.

A burst of gunfire suddenly erupted as Colt entered the hallway ahead of them, exploding the chandelier that hung in the open stairwell and then shattering a large vase in front of them. Pieces of wood from the balcony rail and shards of glass splintered and flew in every direction. Blake pushed Cait down to the right and lay on top of her while Colt dove to the left to distract the shooter.

"His bodyguards." Cait could barely get the words out with Blake's weight on her. "Five."

Blake keyed his mic. "Five bodyguards. Repeat, five bodyguards." Another wave of gunfire ensued, with the suppressed sound of Colt's gun now joining the cacophony of the automatic weapons.

Blake turned his head enough to see Colt standing calmly erect at the top of the stairs, exposed and fearless, aiming and firing as serenely as if he were hunting squirrels, while anyone who dared move forward fell from his marksmanship.

Suddenly, all was quiet again.

"Copy that." Colt's voice came over the radio, composed and unruffled. "Four confirmed down."

Knowing there was still another bodyguard somewhere in the house, Blake and Colt moved cautiously but swiftly. As quiet as the house had become, the noise on the outside had done nothing but intensify. It sounded like a major battle was taking place on the grounds of the compound, and it was growing louder and more concentrated by the minute.

A movement out of the corner of Blake's eye caused him to push Caitlin roughly to the floor. "Tango, five o'clock." Both men hit the ground and rolled to their right, firing when they saw the man crouched in the doorway taking aim. He dropped the gun before falling face first onto the floor.

"And that makes five." The words were said in a matter-of-fact tone without a wasted word, movement, or breath. "House clear."

Colt took the lead then, his gun still rotating from left to right, alert and ready for an attack from any direction. When he reached the door, he turned and motioned for Cait to lie low and to the side, out of harm's way. "Wait for my signal to come out." He had to practically yell over the din of gunfire. Making sure Blake understood, he held up the okay signal. Then a thumbs up. That's when Blake noticed a discolored blotch on Colt's right side, just beneath his body armor.

He grabbed Colt's arm before he opened the door. "Whoa. You're hit, man. You stay here with Cait. I'll go."

"Fuck off. I'm fine." Colt disappeared through the door as a new barrage of gunfire ensued.

As Blake took a knee by the door, waiting for the okay to

bring Cait out, he noticed a dark spot on the floor. Unable to see what it was through his night vision goggles, he touched it with his gloved hand, and then brought his finger closer to his eye. Blood. And there was a puddle of it.

He knew then with certainty, Colt was not fine.

Chapter 34

Just as Blake had predicted, the easy part was over. Now it was time to evacuate. In his mind's eye, he could see a clock ticking, and was beginning to feel anxious about the volume of gunfire. At this point, they had no idea how many fighters were out there, where they were coming from, or how to stop them.

Blake concentrated on the voices coming over his earpiece. Everyone seemed to be engaged in a gunfight, and it didn't sound like there was any diminishing the enemy's numbers. They just kept coming.

There was always a predictable dance and rhythm of battle, a surge and violent wave of motion and noise that would be inexplicably and suddenly reduced to almost perfect stillness. In this case, they seemed to be having trouble getting to the stillness part. They needed more manpower.

Blake flicked on his mic. "Thunderbolt to Fury One."

No answer.

"Thunderbolt to Fury One. Come in. Over."

He heard the voice of Wes instead of Colt.

"Raptor Two to Thunderbolt. I'm seeing movement from a building about a click east of your location. Two pickup trucks full of tangos heading your way."

"Copy that," Blake said, giving a worried glance back toward Cait.

"Heavily armed, Thunderbolt. Mounted guns. Probably 50-cals." After about thirty seconds of silence, Wes came back on the radio. "We're moving into position. Requesting permission to engage."

"Permission granted," Blake answered mechanically without taking his eyes off Cait. She looked scared, but she nodded as if she knew he had to go. He crawled over to her, staying low. "I have to find Colt." He mouthed the words more than said them because it was like whispering into a hurricane. Then he moved in closer and talked into her ear, keeping his voice calm and steady as if there was no reason for panic. "It's all good. We'll get you out of here."

She gave him the okay sign and a thumbs up just as she had seen Colt do, and even forced a smile, but it was clear she knew he was lying. She knew he wouldn't leave her here unprotected unless things had gone from bad to worse.

He maneuvered her to a place beneath the large, open stairwell where she'd be protected from gunfire and from being seen, yet she had a clear view of anyone entering through two separate doors. No one would be able to sneak up on her, and she'd be protected from the hell that was breaking loose on the outside.

Blake pulled a sidearm out of his vest and handed it to her. He didn't speak. There was nothing to say. He just stared into her steady brown eyes.

He keyed his mic and tried one last time. "Thunderbolt to Fury One." He waited for a response but it didn't come. The firing in front had slowed somewhat, but the flank had grown to a ferocious level. Giving Cait a thumbs up, Blake opened the door and slid outside into the darkness and the danger.

He didn't look back at his wife. He couldn't. He'd already promised himself he would never leave her again. But his teammates were in trouble. His best friend was bleeding. He had to do something.

They were no longer fighting as part of a rescue—but to survive.

Outside the door lay carnage. Even with the dark sky, Blake could see black smoke drifting upward and pools of haze wafting over the ground from the high volume of gunfire. Sticking to the shadows and the protective walls of the house, he crawled toward an area in the yard that was alive with muzzle flashes. He found a group of his men firing away at targets, along with Colt leaning with his back against a low stone wall, talking on the phone with one arm draped across his stomach. Other than the large splotch of blood staining his shirt, he seemed the same as always. Calm. Alert. Watchful. Ready.

When he looked up and noticed Blake, he pulled his knees to his chest and tried to look nonchalant. He was clearly aware of Blake's visual examination of him, but didn't want to acknowledge it.

He pulled the phone away from ear. "Where's Cait?"

"I left her inside. Seemed a little hot out here. You too busy talking to your girlfriend to answer comm?" He winked at his own joke then got serious. "You got a sitrep?"

"Yeah. They just keep coming. We don't know from

where. Perimeters are locked down according to both our guys and the feds. Some of our men are pinned down and have fire coming from all directions."

Colt's eyes were calm. His tone was low and relaxed, as if merely discussing a traffic jam at rush hour. This was a man who had seen everything. Nothing seemed to faze him, and his next words confirmed that position. "Just another day in paradise, bro."

Blake remained quiet as he took in the bad news and watched Colt put the phone back to his ear. They were being flanked and probably surrounded. They needed to stop the flow. He couldn't think of words to describe the menacing hum-whistle that seemed to surround him and be everywhere, yet emanated from no single place in particular.

Ten minutes earlier, getting out was the goal. But now, just to hold their ground and stay alive seemed success enough.

"You okay?" Despite the position Colt now sat in, he could not hide the ever-increasing wet stain on the front of his shirt.

"Never been better." Colt lowered the phone and cocked his head, eyeing Blake with his usual coolness. "Embracing the suck, man."

He put the phone back to his ear. "What the fuck did you just say?" Then, "That's what I thought you said."

He pulled the phone away and spoke to Blake. "There's a chopper coming in soon."

"That's good."

"No. It's not. It's CNN."

"You're shitting me."

"No. Our friend at Homeland gave them the o—"

Gunfire suddenly erupted from inside the house, bringing the conversation to an immediate halt. Neither man hesitated or even paused to figure out what was happening. Both half crawled, half-sprinted through a hail of bullets to the porch.

Colt swung the door open, and Blake entered with his gun in position, seeking targets. His gaze fell upon Cait, still sitting under the stairwell, but with the gun pointing toward a ceiling-to-floor bookcase that was swung open to reveal a door. Two bodies were lying on the floor just on the other side of the threshold, in positions that showed they had intended to walk through but hadn't made it.

She held her finger to her mouth so they wouldn't talk.

"How many?" Blake mouthed the words.

She put her hand in the air and then pointed down with a swooping motion.

"Tunnel?"

She nodded.

Colt keyed his mic. "This is Fury One. We have a tunnel in the house."

Blake leaned toward him. "Want a flash bang?"

"Fuck the flash bang." Colt shook his head. "I'm going to use something that will kill 'em."

"That's my man." Blake gave him a thumb's up. "Go big or go home."

Colt nodded toward Blake, who covered him with his weapon as he walked toward the door. He gave the grenade a toss and closed the door, sprinted to where Blake had covered Caitlin with his body, and dove beside them. The muffled sound of an explosion was followed by a puff of smoke and dust billowing around the edges of the door.

"I want to go home," Cait said when Blake rolled off of her.

Suddenly there was a tremendous crash as plaster rained down from the ceiling and walls, causing the room to fill with a hazy curtain of dust. Alarms sounded, ominous and loud.

Geezuz" Blake said into his mic as he rolled back onto Cait to protect her from the falling debris. "Was that an RPG?"

Another loud explosion resounded as a second rocket hit the upper floor. More dust. More alarms.

"Affirmative." Colt was standing up already, and looking toward the stairs. "The second floor is on fire. We need to get out."

Blake heard the crackling sound of flames as Colt said the words. Already, thick black smoke was tumbling down the stairs in large black waves and filling the room. He could smell it. He could taste it. Rolling off Cait and pulling her to her feet in one movement, he moved toward the door, but the gunfire outside increased at that moment as if to warn them that they would find no safety in that direction.

"*Señora*. This way. Come with me."

All three looked up at the Hispanic woman, and then their eyes dropped to the young boy, clinging to her side.

"Don't hurt this woman." Cait's voice was loud, clearly heard above the din of the gunfire outside.

"That's entirely up to her." Colt's eyes never left the woman's face and his gun was in ready position. "Who is she?"

"Maria. She helped bring me here."

Blake's weapon rose just a little as well, and his finger moved to the trigger.

"No. They made her do it! Threatened her family."

Maria spoke directly to Cait as she wrapped a shirt around her son's face. "*Señora*, I know of a tunnel. A way out. We must hurry."

"We just blew the tunnel." Colt's tone suggested he didn't believe her.

"Not that one. There is another."

Blake and Colt looked at each other, and then Blake turned to Cait. "You trust her? This could be a trap."

"Yes, I trust her." Cait began coughing, giving them all a sense of urgency.

"Let's go." Colt motioned for Maria to walk in front of him. "I see anything I don't like, you're dead. Understand?"

She nodded, visibly trembling. "*Sí, señor*. I understand. I want to take my son away from here."

The sound of a helicopter could be heard overhead, followed by more gunfire. Colt spoke into his mic. "Phantom Force, fall back and begin exfil. Repeat, begin exfil."

The reply of "Roger that," was repeated by the men, with no diminishment in the sound level from outside. The hostage rescue team and an array of federal agencies were apparently now in the fight, causing an even more chaotic scene. Colt was glad his men were fading away.

Chapter 35

Colt didn't like relying on the Mexican woman, but he didn't see that he had much choice. He brought up the rear as Maria led them through a maze of rooms, her son clinging to her leg all the while.

"This way." She turned around and motioned for them as the smoke, and now even the flames, seemed to flow and follow them. Just as they entered a narrow hallway, another RPG rocked the house. As Maria stopped and wrapped her arms around her son, the entire group ran into one another.

"Keep moving." Colt shouted above the noise as the lights flickered and went out so that the only illumination came from the dancing, popping fire that seemed to be nipping at his heels. He was accustomed to operating on battlefields, but the sounds and the shadows the flames created were disturbing and unnerving.

No longer able to see, Colt now relied on Blake's voice and directions, and the sound of Maria as she tried to console her son. After running through a short walkway, they stacked up on each other again when stopped by a closed door. Maria grabbed the handle and shook it desperately, seemingly surprised that it was locked.

"Move away." Colt cleared a path, and gave the door a solid kick. It buckled but did not give.

Maria covered her face with her hands and cried, "It is the only way out."

Colt gave the door another kick and then rammed it with his shoulder, causing it to burst open beneath his weight. He found himself in a small gazebo-type structure that was only about a dozen feet wide. The smoke had not reached here yet, but right outside the constant mutterings of gunfire had not ceased—or even slowed.

Colt glanced around the room. There were no doors. This was a dead end. Maybe a trap.

He started to raise his weapon, but Maria stepped to the center of the room and pushed away a large planter that held an exotic-looking tree.

"This way." She bent over and pulled away a rug.

Blake pushed her out of the way and opened the trap door, then shone a light down the hole.

"I'll go first."

"No, I'll go down first," Colt said. "You bring up the rear. Cait and the woman in the middle."

Colt climbed down the ladder and then shined his light ahead of him, his gun at the ready. It was pretty luxurious for a tunnel. The floor was tile, the walls plastered and painted with ornate wood cornices over each support beam. There appeared to be rooms on each side—probably safe rooms and extra arms and ammunition for the rat to escape an attack.

"It's clear." Colt signaled with his flashlight for Blake to send Caitlin and the others. He felt a huge sense of relief that they were actually going to get everyone out alive, and that thought caused his mind to drift again.

He waited for the banging in his head to clear before opening his eyes. The glaring fluorescent tube over his head made an irritating buzzing noise that added to the hum that whirred in his ears. He brought his hand up to his eyes, trying to blot out both the light and the sound.

"You awake?" The worried face of Blake bending over him came into focus.

Colt swiped the sweat out of his eyes and blinked, searching over Blake's shoulder to see if there was anyone with him. "Where is...?"

Blake put his hand on his shoulder but didn't say anything.

Rising anger at his silence drove drums to bang against Colt's brain. "How bad is it, dammit," he croaked, wincing at the pain.

There was a long, pregnant pause. "She's gone, brother."

Chapter 36

B y the time Blake emerged from the underground tunnel, emergency vehicles were already in place to take Cait and Maria to a hospital to be checked out. Blinking against the sun that had since risen, Blake saw Colt standing with a sat-phone to his ear, nodding his head, deep in conversation.

"I'll be right back, baby." Blake helped Cait into the waiting ambulance and walked over to Colt. "POTUS?" He mouthed the words.

Colt nodded, his jaw set in such a way that let Blake know the news on the other end wasn't good.

"Thanks, buddy." Blake held out his hand and mouthed the words. "For everything."

Colt grasped the extended hand with a firm shake and gazed at Blake with a look as intent as a sniper's aim. "Excuse me one moment, Mr. President," he said before lowering the phone and pressing it against his body. "Told you it would all work out." He winked, his grimy, soot-covered face showing the creases of his smile.

Blake took the opportunity to throw his free arm around Colt in a genuine man-hug. "Thanks for giving me my life back," he said in Colt's ear. "I can never repay you for this."

"Just go live happily ever after." Colt gave him one good slap on the back and took a step back, obviously not comfortable with the attention. "That's payment enough."

Feeling dampness from the close contact, Blake pointed to Colt's bloodied shirt. "You sure you're good to go? Looks like you need to get checked out."

Colt looked down at the red blotch as if he'd forgotten all about the injury he'd received. "Just got sliced open by a piece of that chandelier. A few stitches on the plane ride back, and I'll be good as new." He pointed to the phone. "I gotta go."

Blake nodded. "Okay. Be safe, brother."

"I'd rather be deadly." Colt winked again before bringing the phone up to his ear and walking away.

Blake watched contemplatively as Colt nodded and talked in hushed tones with one arm draped across his stomach, his hand pressing against his shirt as if to ease a pain he wouldn't admit was there. It was clear this incident was just another mission that was now in Colt's past—he was already onto the next one. It was impossible to know how many lives he had saved over the years, and how many he would save in the future. Colt was an authority on the nation's enemies and how to kill them. He was a man who had a natural affinity for violence—some might even say a *desire* for it.

Thank God. Because men like him kept the country safe.

Blake sat on the edge of the hospital bed with Cait practically in his lap. She wouldn't let go.

"I can't wait to see the kids. Are you sure they are okay?"

"You talked to them on the phone. Didn't they sound okay to you?"

"Yes." She sighed. "It seems like it's been months since I last saw them—not days. I was really worried about Whitney."

"She's been worried about you too, but once she sees you again, she'll be fine." Blake gave her a squeeze. "Speaking of worried—I'm glad to hear everything seems to have checked out okay with you too."

She nodded with her head against his chest. "I can go as soon as the release paperwork comes through—so stop stressing."

"That's impossible." He pulled her out to arm's length. "You'll be lucky if I ever let you out of my sight again."

Caitlin put her hands on his face. "You've always taken good care of me. You don't need to change anything. I hope you know that."

When he remained silent, she seemed to want to change the subject. "Where's Maria? Have you seen her?"

"She's fine—going to live with her sister in Houston. She told me to tell you 'thanks.'"

Cait inhaled and sighed. "That's nice."

Blake wrapped her in his arms again and laid his cheek on her head. "I'm so lucky to have you back, Mrs. Madison."

"No. I'm the lucky one." She snuggled in close. "I'm married to the best man in the whole, wide world."

"Ah… speaking of which." He rubbed her back as he talked. "What do you want for our anniversary? Anything. A trip to Jamaica. Paris. Anywhere you want to go. Anything you want to do. It's yours."

Cait looked up at him. "Don't laugh, but first of all I want to go to a hairdresser and get rid of this color before anyone else sees it."

His gaze shifted to her short, dark, hair, and then nodded. "We can make that happen. What else?"

"I want to go back to Hawthorne and spend a quiet, normal day with you and the kids." She put his face in her hands. "And then I want to have the biggest freaking party anyone has ever seen so I can personally thank anyone who had anything to do with this. I know there were a lot of them."

Blake put his head back and smiled. "That's doable, too. Except for Colt."

"How is he? Have you talked to him?"

"Not since this morning."

"Is he here in the hospital? Go get him."

Blake remained quiet a moment, trying to figure out how much he should say. "No, he's not in the hospital."

"So he was treated and released? Call him. I want to talk to him."

Blake decided it was best to reason with her. "You know how Colt is, right?"

Cait's face scrunched in confusion. "What do you mean?"

"He's a tough guy. He got patched up in the field and was sent somewhere else."

"Somewhere else? What are you talking about? The man was bleeding profusely. He needs time to recover. Why can't they send someone else?"

"Because... "

"Because why?"

"Because there is no other Colt. That's all."

She grew quiet, her mind obviously working. "It must be something important."

"Yes. It's pretty important."

Cait swallowed hard. "Something you'd probably like to be part of."

Blake squeezed her. "I've been out of that business for a while. You know that."

"That doesn't mean you don't miss it."

"Colt can handle it."

"But he was wounded."

"His injuries weren't life threatening." Blake paused. "Truth is, if someone would have tried to keep him in the hospital—*that* would have been life threatening."

Cait shook her head. "Blake, I saw the blood. It looked bad."

"No. Just a sliver of that crystal chandelier sliced him open pretty good. Couple dozen stitches and a pint or two of blood on the plane ride back and he'll be ready to roll."

"Poor Colt."

"Poor Colt? How about poor Cait?" His voice turned low and gravely. "I know you've been through hell."

She closed her eyes as if that would help her look to the future, not the past, and slid her hand onto her stomach. "We made it through okay."

He leaned forward, his face just inches from hers and put his hand on hers. "I can't wait. You know that, right?"

When she opened her eyes, they were brimming with tears. "I do now."

She reached up and ran her fingers through his hair and

then looked him in the eyes. "So that's what I want for our anniversary. What do *you* want?"

"You really have to ask?" His steady blue eyes bore into her just before he shot her a sly, sexy grin.

"Besides *that*."

"Just you."

"You're batting a hundred today as far as the title of husband goes."

"I'm good like that." He drew her close and closed his eyes, as if he never needed another thing in his life.

"But it's a big day. There must be something special you want."

He closed his eyes as if concentrating. "Okay. I just now thought of something."

She looked at him with sparkling, anxious eyes. "What?"

"I want to…" He paused a moment as he dug around in his pocket.

"What?" She punched him on the shoulder. "You want to…what?"

"Okay, I'm getting to it. I want to"—he held out his hand—"see your face when you lay your eyes on this."

She shifted her gaze to his open hand, and her eyes instantly glistened with tears again when she saw her wedding band lying there. "How did you…?"

"Magic."

Caitlin continued to stare at it with a look on her face that reflected astonishment mixed with relief and overwhelming happiness.

"Here. Let me put it on."

She held out her left hand, and he slipped it on her trembling finger. "With this ring I thee wed, and with all my love I thee endow." His voice faltered at the end, but he got through it.

"Complete, beautiful, and endless," she said in a whisper, finishing their vow from a year earlier and running her finger across the band.

He gazed into her eyes. "One year together—and many more to come."

"Many, *many* more." She wrapped her arms around him and held him even tighter. "But this is one we're never going to forget."

When Blake remained silent, she pulled slightly away. "You okay?"

"Yeah." He blinked to make sure the tears that threatened did not fall. "I'm okay."

She laid her head against his chest again, and he whispered in her ear. "But I have to tell you, baby, I missed you too much."

The End

FIND OUT WHAT HAPPENS to Colt when he rushes to DC to stop a terrorist attack and meets his match—and his future—in FRONT LINE!

FRONT LINE

Phantom Force Tactical

(Book 3)

Coming December, 2016

EXCERPT:

"How much ammo do you have?"

Nickolas "Colt" Colton looked down at the woman sitting on the floor with her back against the wall beside him. Despite the fact that she was still trying to catch her breath from running up the stairs, her voice sounded casual, like she was asking if he'd brought an umbrella in case of rain.

"Enough for a while. Why?" He knew something was wrong, because up until now everything she'd said had been with a smile and a sense of humor. Her creased brow and serious expression showed no trace of that anymore.

"Because if things go south, I'd appreciate it if you would save one for me." She looked up, forcing Colt to gaze straight into her mesmerizing green eyes. "Okay?"

For a moment, all Colt could do was stare. He had never seen eyes so beautiful and vibrant. Maybe that's why he was so slow to grasp that they belonged to a woman who had just politely asked him to put a bullet through her head if the terrorists got through the door...

Other Books by Jessica James

Historical Fiction

Noble Cause (Heroes Through History Book 1)
(An alternative ending to Shades of Gray)
Above and Beyond (Heroes Through History Book 2)
Liberty and Destiny (Heroes Through History Book 3)
Shades of Gray

Romantic Suspense

Dead Line (Phantom Force Tactical Book 1 – Prequel)
Fine Line (Phantom Force Tactical Book 2)
Front Line (Phantom Force Tactical Book 3)

Non-Fiction

The Gray Ghost of Civil War Virginia: John Singleton Mosby
From The Heart: Love Stories and Letters of the Civil War

About the Author:

Jessica James is an award-winning author of military fiction and non-fiction ranging from the Revolutionary War to modern day. She is the only two-time winner of the John Esten Cooke Award for Southern Fiction, and was featured in the book *50 Authors You Should Be Reading,* published in 2010.

Her novels appeal to both men and women and are featured in library collections all over the United States including Harvard and the U.S. Naval Academy. By weaving the principles of courage, devotion, duty, and dedication into each book, she attempts to honor the unsung heroes of the American military—past and present—and to convey the magnitude of their sacrifice and service.

James is a member of the Romance Writers of America, the Military Writers Society of America, and the Independent Book Publishers Association.

Contact the Author

Email Jessica@JessicaJamesBooks.com
www.JessicaJamesBooks.com

www.Facebook.com/RomanticHistoricalFiction
Twitter: @Jessica James
www.goodreads.com/JessicaJames
www.pinterest.com/southernromance
www.bookbub.com/authors/jessica-james

Awards

2015 Foreword Magazine Book of the Year Finalist

2015 New Jersey Romance Writers Golden Leaf Award

Valley Forge Romance Writers Sheila Award Finalist

2014 John Esten Cooke Award for Southern Fiction

2014 Reader's Crown Award Finalist

2014 Next Generation Indie Award Finalist in Fiction/Religious

2013 USA "Best Books 2013" Finalist in Fiction/Religious

2012 Foreword Magazine Book of the Year (Bronze) in Romance

2011 John Esten Cooke Award for Southern Fiction

2011 USA "Best Books 2011" Finalist in Historical Fiction

2011 Next Generation Indie Award for Best Regional Fiction

2011 Next Generation Indie Finalist in Romance

2011 Next Generation Indie Finalist in Historical Fiction

2011 NABE Pinnacle Book Achievement Award

2010 Stars and Flags Book Award in Historical Fiction

2009 HOLT Medallion Finalist for Best Southern Theme

2009 Nominated for the Michael Shaara Award for Excellence in Civil War Fiction

2008 Indie Next Generation Award for Best Regional Fiction

2008 Indie Next Generation Finalist for Best Historical Fiction

2008 IPPY Award for Best Regional Fiction

2008 ForeWord Magazine Book of the Year Finalist in Romance

Made in the USA
Coppell, TX
08 May 2021